MW01595123

Brushed Away

Jason Deas

Ball Ground, Georgia, USA

3-Day Ranch Press

Cover Art: Keri Knutson

This one is for my wife, Karen. Thanks for letting me spend so much time with Benny James and the gang.

"All good things got to come to an end
The thrills have to fade
Before they come 'round again"

Jackson Browne

Chapter 1

The houseboat rocked. Benny popped up from his nap. Peering out the window, he saw a speedboat breaking the "no wake" rule. Benny wondered where the boat might be coming from in such haste. He plopped back down in bed. Benny's head ached. His girlfriend of a year and a half, Rachael, had dumped him with no warning for a chance at an international media gig in London. After her call, Benny had four too many drinks.

Benny heard feet pounding down the dock and knew he was needed. Fists rained down on his door.

"Get out here now, Benny," yelled the marina owner Donny.

Benny ran to the door and pulled it open.

"Something sick happened at Rene's."

"What?"

"Somebody hung a painting of blood."

"What do you mean it was made of blood?"

"Instead of using paint, the artist used blood."

"How did they get inside?"

"The person didn't break in, they did it while Rene was open. They did it this morning. I guess the employees were in the back or something and the guy hung it and left."

"Did Rene call Vernon and Chuckie?"

Benny had a history with the Chief of police, Chief Charles "Chuckie" Neighbors. Benny was not a big fan of his ability to try women on like clothes.

"You know Chuckie," Donny said, "he threw up when he saw the blood."

Not only was Charles a man-whore, he was also one of the worst lawmen in the country. Benny had worked a previous case with him and he had thrown up all over one of the crime scenes.

"Contaminated the scene again?"

"He did."

"Is Vernon there?"

"Yeah. He asked me to get you. He said you wouldn't answer your phone."

Vernon was the backbone of the Tilley police department. He handled all things above speeding tickets and petty crimes. Tilley, Georgia was a very small town and not used to things out of the ordinary. A couple years back, the town had exploded onto the national scene with a case that grabbed the country's attention, but since the case had been solved it had slowed back down to a sleepy dot on the map.

"You smell like a brewery," Donny said cupping one hand over his nose.

"I have to brush my teeth and I'll be on my way."

Benny arrived at Rene's ten minutes later. A small crowd had gathered outside the restaurant. The waiters, waitresses, and patrons were on the front patio giving statements to deputies. One of the young waitresses was convulsed with emotion and Benny got down on one knee in front of her.

"Listen here, doll. Everything's going to be OK." Benny carefully put one hand on her shoulder. "Are you scared?"

"Yes."

"It's normal. You've been a part of something frightening. My name is Benny James."

The young waitress looked up.

"I know who you are."

"I'm going to find whoever did this. I promise you that."

"OK."

"I'm going inside now to take a look. Are you going to be OK?"

"I think so."

"I think so, too."

The young waitress grabbed Benny's neck and gave him one of the strongest hugs he had ever experienced. Benny hugged back and felt her relax. When he let go her crying had stopped.

"My mom was supposed to pick me up after my shift and she's not answering the phone. My shift wasn't supposed to end for five more hours."

"If you don't get her on the phone by the time I come out, I'll give you a ride home. What's your name?"

"Angel."

"Really?"

"My parents were, are, hippies."

"All right, Angel. Don't fly away."

An officer was guarding the door and let Benny enter the restaurant. Inside, Chief Neighbors sat at a table nursing a Sprite, still looking nauseous.

Vernon had his face about an inch from the painting with his back to the entrance.

"Is tonight the opening for the blood and guts series?" Benny joked.

Vernon turned, looking like he might follow Chief Neighbor's lead and throw up as well. He swatted flies away from his face. A swarm of them had recently found the painting.

"How can you make jokes?"

"Vernon, I know you don't want to believe it, but this is just another day at the office for me. I might have to find myself another sleepy town to retire in if this keeps happening."

Chief Neighbors took a deep breath and looked up from his Sprite. "How can we be sure that it's blood?"

"Do you usually throw up when you see red paint?" Benny asked. "Do flies like red paint? This is fresh, Chuckie. I know you haven't seen or smelled much blood in your life, but this is blood. I can assure you of that."

"Would it kill you to call me Chief?"

"It might."

"I heard you call me Chief Asshole behind my back."

"Who told you that?"

"I heard you say it once."

"Oh."

"What would it take from me to get you to stop that?"

"Ten days."

"What do you mean by ten days?"

"Remember the last murder case you had in your town? You gave Vernon and me ten days to solve it before you requested outside help. Give us the same deal and I will never call you Chief Asshole again."

"Deal," Chief Neighbors said.

"Deal." Benny grabbed his hand to authenticate the gentleman's agreement.

"How do we even know a crime has been committed?" Chief Neighbors asked. "I don't think it's a crime to paint with blood and nobody broke in the café."

"There is a body that goes with this," Benny said. "Don't you think so Vernon?"

"Oh yeah. I'm no art critic, but those strokes show real anger. Somebody is definitely dead." Vernon held his breath and took another close look at the canvas. "The artist wrote all over here with a pen or marker. Look at all these tiny numbers. He wrote the number four all over the place."

Benny arched his neck toward the painting and narrowed his eyes. "He must have written the number four on here a hundred times or more."

"What do you think it means?" Vernon backed away again from the painting.

"I have no idea, but let's cover all our simple bases first. Somebody needs to check room four at the Lakeside Motor Inn and the Tuck 'Em Inn. I don't know if storage units have numbers on them, but if they do we need to look inside of the ones labeled four."

"Mile marker four is by a pretty heavily wooded area," Vernon said. "Somebody needs to check the woods around there."

Chief Neighbors piped in saying, "The campground has site numbers. I think I might have had a little tryst on that exact site. Stay away from the picnic table."

"I guess you're feeling better?" Benny asked.

"I think it was Katrina or her sister Cameron. We were in the tent the whole time, except of course when we were on the picnic table."

"Chief," Benny said. "We're working a case here, not reminiscing about your exploits."

"Of course." Chief Neighbors stood up. I gotta go call Katrina or Cameron, or both. I hope they didn't get married since the last time I saw them."

"Doesn't really matter does it?" Benny asked.

Chief Neighbors didn't get the shot Benny had just taken at him as he answered, "I don't guess it does. Get to work boys."

"He's a real piece of work," Vernon laughed.

"He's something."

Benny saw what he needed to see inside the restaurant and left. The crowd outside had thinned. Angel was still there and waiting under one of the outdoor umbrellas.

"Couldn't get your mom on the phone?" Benny questioned as he approached her.

"No. She's probably in her studio, painting. She doesn't like to be interrupted when she's painting."

"She doesn't paint with blood, does she?" Benny asked, only half joking.

"She's weird, but she's not that weird."

Once in his Jeep, Benny told Angel to buckle up.

"I haven't seen you around town before," he said as Angel pointed which way to go.

"I've served you and Officer Kearns before. Twice actually. I've even babysat Vernon's twins once or twice."

"Of course," Benny said peering over at Angel, taking a long look. The Jeep swerved and his eyes found the road again. "Did you get a haircut?"

"Yeah. And I dyed it black."

"I like it."

"I thought most men preferred blondes?"

"Not me," Benny said.

Angel laughed. "I don't really care what most men like."

"Oh?" Benny thought she was getting at the fact that she liked girls, which he thought was too intimate a subject for virtual strangers.

"Boys my age are just a bunch of dumbasses."

"Seems like you've got teenaged boys pegged pretty well."

Angel pointed again and Benny turned down a dirt road. "Only place down this road is the old Oglethorpe plantation. Or what used to be the Oglethorpe plantation."

"That's me. Angel Oglethorpe."

"Oh my God."

"The cool way to say it now is omigod," Angel suggested.

"Omigod," Benny repeated.

Angel threw her head back with laughter. "Now you got it. Do you know the history of this piece of land?"

"I think everybody in town does. Your great grandfather was one of the richest men in this part of the country."

"He was actually my great, great grandfather. He had over four thousand acres of land and grew everything from cotton to pecans to peaches."

"All the Georgia staples."

"You better believe it. The plantation house was magnificent back in its day. There are still a few oil paintings of it in the house. It's all pretty dilapidated now."

"Nobody really knows what happened. It seems to be a mystery how your family lost its fortune."

"Nobody knew how to run the business once my great, great grandfather died. He had an amazing drive for business and he didn't pass it on to anyone. He thought he was the only person who could do anything right, and he never asked anybody for help. In turn, he didn't teach anybody how to run the business and when he died the business slowly died as well. The money lasted for a while, but eventually ran out. Through the years almost all the original land had to be sold. Out of the four thousand acres, we now only own twenty."

Once on Oglethorpe land, Benny's Jeep drove past giant metal sculptures sprouting from the earth as if they were living entities. Benny stopped next to one. "That looks like a weeping willow made of rusted metal. Very cool."

"My Uncle Karl made that and all the other yard sculptures you'll see. He's crazy as hell, but talented."

"Do you have a lot of artists in the family?"

"No. Just Mom and Uncle Karl. It's just the three of us living in the house now."

"If I remember correctly, that's a pretty big house for three people."

"Most of the rooms are closed off. Mom is always in her studio and Uncle Karl basically lives in his art barn out back. That's my favorite of Uncle Karl's sculptures," Angel said pointing.

Benny stopped the Jeep again and looked. "That's incredible. How did he do that?"

"I told you he was talented."

Standing forty feet tall was an almost perfect replica of a bird. The crane peered down toward the ground. The bird crooked one of its legs in the air revealing a beautifully crafted webbed foot. The massive bird appeared to be fishing.

Benny drove his Jeep up the circular drive in front of the house and stopped at the large front door.

"Thanks for the ride."

"Not a problem."

"Tell Red I said hello."

"How do you know Red?"

"Uncle Karl gets tomatoes from him. He brought Red over here one day last week. He talked about you a lot. Red ended up buying one of Uncle

Karl's sculptures and they installed it by Red's garden a few days ago."

"I have got to see this." Benny chuckled to himself as he drove away from the house and toward Red's.

Chapter 2

Benny spotted Red in his garden. His cat Galaxie followed one step behind. Red spent most of his time in his garden and he sometimes even napped among his plants. Red had been raised by deaf-mute parents away from the world in the Ozark Mountains. He spoke like a drunk five-year-old and had the innocent heart of a child. He had arrived on Benny's doorstep a few years earlier and Benny loved everything about him and looked after him like a father would his own son.

"Bendy," Red hollered as he spotted the Jeep in his driveway.

As Benny walked toward him he noticed the large sculpture behind him.

"Does you seeing my art. Red now liking art."

"It would be hard to miss," Benny said studying the piece.

"It a sea aminal with super light power."

"I see."

At the back of Red's garden stood a giant metal sea creature, almost as high as the house that looked like a mutation of an octopus. Instead of eight arms, Benny quickly counted a dozen or more snaking in all directions. Attached to each of the arms were thousands upon thousands of tiny mirrors. Light reflected from the piece and from some angles Benny thought it was almost painful to view.

"The vegables thanking me every day for this."

"Let me guess," Benny said. "They like all the extra light?"

"Yep. You smart man, Bendy."

"I don't mean to pry into your personal business," Benny started, "but how much did you pay for this?"

Benny had collected five hundred thousand dollars for Red a few years earlier and wanted to make sure Karl had not found out about his money and trying to take advantage of him.

"It costed a thousand tomatoes."

"You didn't give Karl any money?"

"Nope. He just say I owe him a thousand tomatoes."

"You're quite the business man. I didn't know you were selling your vegetables? You always give me stuff for free."

"That because you Red bestest friend."

Benny beamed.

His thoughts turned to the bloody canvas and he wondered if Karl might be weird enough to pull off such a sick stunt. Red was usually a pretty good judge of character.

"Tell me about Karl. How did you meet him?"

"Red meeted he at food store. He have tomatoes in he cart and Red tell he not to buying they yucky tomato."

"When was this?"

"Same day I call you on talky machine about bombs."

Red's house was located less than a mile from Tilley's main park where the city put on a spectacular fireworks show every Fourth of July.

The first year Red had been in the house he called Benny terrified, thinking the world was coming to an end. As Red did not keep up with the date, he called Benny every Fourth of July when the fireworks started to tell him about the bombs. Benny always had to remind him that it was the day America celebrated its independence by shooting fireworks. Red always laughed and said he thought it was silly to celebrate by making loud noises.

"Can you keep a secret, Red?"

"You know Red can." Red's face hardened.

Benny put a hand on his shoulder and said, "I'm sorry I even asked. I know you can keep a secret. I can't think of anybody in this world I trust more than you." Red smiled, his demeanor back to normal. "Something bad happened this morning at Rene's."

"You face looking worry."

"I am worried, buddy. Somebody hung a painting in Rene's made of blood, and I'm afraid we're going to find a body that goes with it."

"It good it happen here," Red said.

"Why is that?"

"Because you here," Red said incredulously. "You find any bad mans. Red knowing you be finding this bad man too."

"Thanks, buddy."

"Next time Karl come for he tomatoes, Red will integrate he."

"You'll interrogate him for me?"

"Red will."

"You're the best. Be cool though. Don't let him know what's going on."

"Red be cool."

"Keep your eyes open, buddy."

"Red eyes always open unless Red being asleep."

"Very good," Benny said trying the best he could to conceal the smile trying to flash across his face.

When Benny's cell phone rang as he was driving, he knew it was bad news.

"It's the campground," Vernon said. "Site number four."

"On my way." Benny tossed the phone on the seat next to him and stomped on the gas pedal. As he sped down the country roads, his thoughts slipped to Rachael as he wondered what she was doing. He calculated what time it was in London. Benny had not been dumped many times in his life besides Jane, and it hurt. He pushed the gas pedal all the way to the floor. With his left hand, Benny let all the windows down and felt the rush of air and the dangerous speed in which he was travelling wash over him. He let the thought of Rachael fall to the roadside, and he readied his mind for the crime scene awaiting him.

Benny drove the Jeep into the Talking Pines Campground. Vernon already had the entrance to the campground blocked and guarded. Officer Andy Mandelino waved him through.

As he motored slowly around toward site number four, he noticed families packing their cars and campers. Benny surmised Vernon had ordered an immediate evacuation of the grounds. Benny wondered what the occupants had been told.

As he approached site four, Benny spied Vernon and the infamous yellow tape signifying a crime scene. Vernon was waiting for Benny. He looked ill.

"You look awfully white for a black man," Benny said as Vernon greeted him with a pair of gloves. Benny slipped the gloves on his hands and took in the scene.

"We've seen some strange, strange stuff together, but this one takes the cake," Vernon said. "We've already photographed extensively around the tent, so it's cool to walk around."

Benny stood still and looked around. A green three-man tent was pitched in the middle of an area filled with pea gravel. Benny searched the pea gravel for footprints and did not find any. He thought it strange.

"Did you look inside?" he asked Vernon.

"Yes, unfortunately."

"Where are your footprints?"

"We put a sheet of plywood down."

Benny smiled and pointed at Vernon. "Is somebody looking for a promotion?"

"Hell no. Only position up from mine is Chief."

"And?"

"Damn. I wouldn't run against Chuckie. And y'all white folks wouldn't vote me in, anyhow."

"You got my vote."

"Thanks. Now stop dreaming and take a look inside the tent."

Benny walked toward the tent door and his head popped back.

"I know what that smell is," he told Vernon.

Benny cupped his hand over his face. He pulled the flap to the side and peered inside. An incredibly large man lay on his back, slashed to pieces. His throat, chest, stomach, and legs suffered small cuts. He was naked. The bottom of the tent had a thin pool of blood, some of which was still not dried. Benny backed out of the tent.

"We got us a first timer," Benny said.

"What do you mean?"

"Whoever did this is a first time killer. I would bet my life on it."

"Why?"

"There is uncertainty in the knife slashes. Our killer didn't know if the ones across his neck would do the job, so they continued and slashed his chest. As he gasped for his last breaths our killer panicked and slashed his stomach and legs. I guarantee you if he hadn't died then, we would be finding more of him carved up."

"Why do people do these things?"

"Rage, money, jealousy." Benny backed away from the tent and tried to shake the smell out of his nostrils. "Too many reasons."

"I'm no expert," Vernon said, "but I don't see rage in those slashes."

"You're right. Now tell me why."

"The cuts aren't deep enough or long enough."

"Right again."

Vernon's chest puffed out a little and he continued. "I can tell the knife he used was incredibly sharp by the flaps of skin. A dull knife would have torn the skin, but those cuts are smooth."

"You're starting to make me feel useless," Benny joked.

"I guess it's like anything, the more you see and experience, the better you become."

"I'm afraid so."

"Come look at this," Vernon said, walking over toward the concrete picnic table.

Benny took a few steps before the tabletop came into view. "Well, that's fresh," he said. "And interesting. What the hell is it?"

Someone had taken a rock or something of the sort and carved an image into the top of the table. The abstract image seemed in places like it would burst into a realistic figure and then it somehow dove back into abstraction. Just as the viewer's eyes recovered from one trick of lines, more pulled the eyes to another section that almost revealed itself, and did not. The artist created a dance for the eyes and a curious journey of near discoveries.

"Is this thing moving?" Benny said as he had to look away.

"I felt the same thing. I thought maybe I was just feeling queasy from what I had seen in the tent."

"Somebody is talented," Benny said. "We need to start looking at artists around town and see if we can match this style. Not just anybody could do *this*."

"If you want to get on that, I'll find out who the guy in the tent is and maybe we can connect the two. I've already asked the camp attendant to give me a printout of all the names, phone numbers, and addresses of people who have been staying here in the last week. I'll get some of the deputies to start visiting or calling all of them to find out if they saw or heard anything."

Benny took two steps back, feigning anger. "You sure you need me?"

Vernon tried to hide his pride and smothered a grin. "You taught me well. I do need you."

"I think I actually need you more than you need me this time around. I need to keep my mind busy."

"What do you mean?"

"Rachael's moving on."

"Shut your mouth! She burned you?"

"Afraid so." Benny's eyes began to well up.

Vernon put a hand on his shoulder and squeezed. "Her loss, my friend. You want to go get a beer?"

"Nah. Thanks though. I just want to try to wrap my mind around this alone today. Maybe tomorrow."

"I understand. Damn! She was a good one, brother."

"She was. And thanks for not talking bad about her. She deserves better than that."

"Yes, she does. Hey, if you get to feeling lonely or need to talk, call or just come on over to the house. We got plenty of commotion to take your mind off your problems."

"The twins doing OK?"

"I'm surprised every day that the house is still standing. The boys are wild. Karma's a mean bitch."

Benny laughed. "Let's touch base later."

"Promise me one thing."

"OK."

"Don't drink this problem away like you did Jane."

Benny had been married to a local named Jane for a short time. She had been Chief Neighbors' high school sweetheart and wife. Jane had hired Benny to find out if Chief Neighbors was cheating on her. After he gave her proof that he was, a romance followed and marriage. Vernon called Benny not long after they tied the knot to let him know that Jane's heart had floated back to the Chief, and Benny busted them in the Chief's office. A divorce and a tight friendship were the results of the secret phone call.

"I won't. I tried it last night and the problem was still here this morning."

"Is that why my phone rang at three o'clock in the morning?"

Benny fanned out both of his hands and shook his head. "Wasn't me."

Chapter 3

Another sun-drenched morning graced the Sleepy Cove Marina. Benny's houseboat gently swayed as the fishing boats headed out. He was not a morning person and usually rolled out of bed around ten. He peeked at the clock and found it to be a few minutes before six. His brain took off and he tried to fall back to sleep without any success. He could not calm his thoughts. Benny cursed and got out of bed.

Although it was four hours earlier than usual, he followed his morning ritual and headed up to the marina's office for the morning paper.

"What's wrong?" Donny yelled when he walked in the door.

"Nothing," Benny tried.

"Aw damn! Does this have anything to do with Rachael not being on TV last night?"

"Maybe."

Donny grabbed his face and pulled the cap off his head. He slammed it to the floor and then kicked it across the room. He put his head down on the counter swearing and hollering indecipherable phrases.

"Whoa! She didn't break up with you. She dumped *me*," Benny said.

"I'm so upset. I feel like I've been kicked in the stomach. I need to sit down." Donny stumbled over to one of the couches lining the walls of the office and bait shop.

"Are you kidding me here? Am I still asleep and dreaming?"

"She didn't just dump you!" Donny screamed. "She dumped this whole town—me included. I don't think I can ever watch that channel again." Donny jumped up and ran toward the television set hanging on the wall across the room. As he neared the set, he jumped as if he was an NBA player about to make a fantastic dunk. With one finger outstretched, he flew through the air and caught the power button. As he landed, the television went dark. "Please go," he told Benny. "I need to be alone."

"Um... OK. Call me if you need a hug," Benny said in jest, picking up the newspaper.

"I do," Donny said, getting up again and walking toward Benny.

Benny threw his hands up not believing the situation. Donny fell into his arms and trembled as he gave Benny a tremendous bear hug.

"You'll get over this," Benny said.

"I won't," Donny answered.

"Give it time."

As Benny left he heard the door lock. When he turned around to see what was going on he saw Donny putting the "Closed" sign in the door window.

Is he for real? Benny thought. He peered at the front page of the paper and the headline read, "Murder. Again." He tucked the paper under his arm and made his way back to the houseboat with *Birdsongs* painted on its stem and stern.

With the coffee maker dripping, Benny read the front page story in the *Tilley Bee* and thought about his old friend Jerry Lee, who at one time wrote for and edited the newspaper. Jerry Lee had been an unusual soul who made up his own curse words, and in honor of him, Benny said aloud to no one, "Peanuts!"

With coffee in hand, Benny sat on the top deck of *Birdsongs* and listened to the morning. He heard a few boat motors coming and going, birds, waves, and his own breathing. He realized that once again, without Rachael, he was alone. He tried to think good thoughts. At forty-nine, he was still in good health. He had fantastic black hair that still curled if grown past a certain point. His chameleon eyes still stopped people on the street. His fit body and deep voice were now back on the market, and if Benny could have heard the undertones of the city, he would have heard the women of Tilley rejoicing.

Benny knew Vernon would be awake and called him after his second cup of coffee.

"What are you doing up so early?" Vernon asked.

"Couldn't sleep."

"You want to get an early start?"

"Might as well," Benny answered.

"Where're you gonna start?"

"Oglethorpe place. I hear two of the residents are artists. Maybe they can tell me where to start."

"I hear the uncle is a crazy old coot."

"You know I love crazies. Did you find anything out about the vic?"

"We're working on it. I'll have something definite by lunch. You want to meet?"

"Yeah. Meet me at the marina at noon and I'll throw something together. Did Rene say when she was going to reopen?"

"Tomorrow. She doesn't think anybody would eat there even if she opened today. She was going to take the week off but said she couldn't afford it. She said the food spoilage alone would cost her a couple thousand dollars. I guess she buys everything fresh. Doesn't she live in the same marina as you?"

"No. She lives across the lake."

"Maybe after lunch we can both go over and talk to her."

"Sounds like a plan."

"See you at noon."

"If I'm not back, just let yourself in with your key and make yourself at home."

"You know I will."

After hanging up the phone, Benny poured himself one more cup of coffee and got ready for the day. On his way to his Jeep, he noticed the sign in Donny's window was still reading "Closed." Benny couldn't help but laugh.

As Benny drove down the Oglethorpe's long dirt drive, he stopped once again to marvel at the giant metal sculptures. Just as he put the vehicle back in gear an animal bolted across the road in front of him and disappeared in between some bushes on the other side. It all happened so fast, Benny couldn't decide what kind of animal it was. He knew it was as tall as a horse, but he could have sworn it stood vertically like a kangaroo or a human. And it was fast! Images of the cartoon Roadrunner flew through his mind, and Benny couldn't help saying aloud, "Beep, beep." *It's going to be a strange day*, he thought.

An older man stood in front of the Oglethorpe house with a worried look on his face. Benny couldn't tell how old he was as his skin was lobster red and glowing with some sort of lotion Benny imagined to be aloe. The man wore overalls without a shirt underneath and as Benny neared, he noticed the man pull a tube of lotion out of his pocket. He squirted some in his hands and rubbed his shoulders and arms. He even rubbed a handful through his white hair, massaging his scalp. The man noticed Benny's Jeep and stuffed the tube of lotion back into his pocket.

Before Benny could even get the car in park, the man was at his door.

"Did you find her?" the man asked.

"Who are we talking about?"

"About this tall," the man said, holding his hand in the air above his head. "Fast as hell. White. Black. Peachy pink."

Benny got out of the Jeep. "We're not talking about a person I assume?"

"Nope. We're talking about Clarice."

"And Clarice is?"

"Shifty."

"And?"

"Lost."

"What kind of animal is Clarice?"

"Ostrich."

"Thank you. I think I may have seen her," Benny said remembering the streak that ran across the road in front of him. "I saw her back by your crane sculpture."

"I knew it," the man said. "She thinks I like her better and she's mad because I wouldn't make her a BLT last night."

"That would make me mad as well. Is there anything I can do to help?"

"Yes. Scream like I'm kicking your ass."

"What?"

"Clarice don't like violence. If she thinks I'm beating you up, she'll come running and knock me over. Then I can apologize and make her a BLT."

"OK," Benny said, wondering if he really was still asleep and dreaming. "How do I start?"

"Just act like I'm hitting you and kicking you over and over again."

"OK." Benny had been in some weird situations before, but he decided this one was even stranger than the day he met Red. He took a deep breath and put on an Oscar worthy performance of having his ass kicked. "Stop! Ouch! Ow!..."

Thirty seconds later a black and white streak tore across the yard and knocked the man in overalls down. The angry ostrich stood over him and glared down into his eyes.

"Tell her you're OK," the man yelled. "And call her by name."

"I'm OK, Clarice. Let him go. Clarice, I'm OK."

The ostrich took a step back as the man got off the ground.

"You are so stubborn," he said to the tall bird. "If you want to eat your friends, then fine, you can have a BLT." The man nodded his head up and down as if the ostrich was talking and he was listening. "I know, pigs are stupid." He listened again and nodded. "Yes, they are delicious and I'm sorry. I won't ever eat a BLT in front of you again without sharing. Will you get back inside the fence now? I have a visitor."

The man turned and walked toward the back of the house and the ostrich followed. Benny followed as well. At the back of the house, the man opened a gate and the ostrich walked inside. The man shut the gate and turned to Benny.

"Thanks," he said pulling the tube of aloe out of his pocket again.

"You're welcome. I'm guessing you're Karl?"

"You can call me Uncle Karl."

"Um... OK."

"Do me a favor," Uncle Karl said. "Put some of this on my back."

Before Benny could object, he squirted a handful of aloe into Benny's hands and turned around. White hairs stood above red skin. Benny took a deep breath and began rubbing.

"Oh yeah," Uncle Karl moaned. "Right there. Oh. Oh. Yeah."

When Benny finished, Uncle Karl turned around and flashed him an unusual smile. Benny thought he was about to speak, but he didn't.

"That's one hell of a sunburn," Benny finally said.

"Arc welder did it."

"What? How?"

"I got drunk last night and decided to weld a few pieces together in my studio. I had my shirt off and forgot that the light from an arc welder is just as bright, or brighter than the sun. Woke up in hell this morning and couldn't figure out what had happened last night. I finally remembered my welding and it all clicked."

"Interesting."

"Who are you anyway?"

"Benny James. I gave Angel a ride home yesterday and she told me you were an artist. I'm also friends with Red."

"Son of a monkey! Red! Any friend of Red's is a friend of mine. That kid grows the best tomatoes this side of the Mississippi. Are you the Benny he talks about?"

"That's me."

"Are you here to steal my ostrich?"

"No. I want some information about art."

"Then you came to the right spot."

Chapter 4

Vernon pored over documents back at
department headquarters. Something did not add
up, and he was miffed. Although he treasured his
friendship with Benny, Vernon dreamed of being his
equal. He knew he would most probably never work
for the FBI, but he knew his mind was sharp, and his
ability to solve crimes was above average. He
wanted to unravel this problem without Benny's
help.

As Vernon waited on an identification of the
victim, the reports from his deputies kept coming in.
It appeared that no one had seen anything. The
camp attendant even assured him after double and
triple checking, that the site was not rented on the
night in question. The camp attendant also
ascertained that the gates to the campground closed
promptly at ten thirty every night, and there was no
possible way to get around the gates without driving
across the site where his personal camper was
parked.

Vernon decided to give him one more call.

"Hello Officer Kearns. Would you like me to
check the registry a fourth time?"

"That won't be necessary," Vernon answered.
"You were telling me earlier that your camper is
parked near the main gate."

"Yes. We close the gates so people can't enter
the park after hours and use the park without
registering. It covers a lot of problems like high
schoolers having parties and leaving before a camp
attendant is on duty. Before the gates, we had a lot

of problems with that. Not only did they not pay, they left all their beer bottles and trash around the sites."

"And you said it's impossible to drive around the gate?"

"No. It's not impossible. Somebody could do it, but if I didn't see it, I'd hear it. Even if they turned out their headlights, I swear to you I would hear it. And if I didn't, my dog would, and she would bark her head off."

"Perfect," Vernon said. "I know how they got in."

"Huh?" the camp attendant asked, but Vernon was already headed to his car.

Vernon knew the campground was still closed, but flew down the roads anyway. His hands tightly gripped the steering wheel as he gritted his teeth with anticipation. His foot that was not on the accelerator tapped with excess energy.

Vernon drove up to the gates of the Talking Pines Campground. Officer Andy Mandelino recognized his car and pulled the gate open.

"What's up Vernon?" Officer Mandelino asked.

"Just had a wild idea," Vernon stated. "I'll radio you in a minute. If what I'm thinking is right, we're going to need to get the team back over here to take some more photos and to collect evidence."

"I hope you're right. I'll be listening."

Vernon parked the car at site number four. Yellow tape still surrounded the camping area. The body, of course, had been removed from the tent, but the tent was still staked to the ground. Vernon had requested a truck to move the tent, not collapsed, to a climate-controlled storage space where it could be kept intact until he decided what to do with the piece of evidence. He felt by collapsing it and rolling it up, it could in some way destroy the integrity of the evidence they may not have uncovered inside. The truck was due within the hour.

Vernon emerged from his vehicle. He viewed the camp site and attempted to see it with new eyes. He stood still and scanned the entire area. After taking in the visual information, his eyes turned toward the water. He looked for the most direct route to the water and slowly walked that way. As he walked, his eyes searched the ground for clues. He veered slightly from the path he thought the killer might have taken so as to avoid disturbing any possible evidence.

At the water's edge, Vernon spied the first bit of visual evidence that told him his hunch was correct. A wide gash in the sand running at least four to five feet onto the beach told him a boat had landed in haste. Most boaters would have eased their vessels onto the beach. This particular boater hit the beach head on at a pretty fast clip. Scanning the ground, he did not find any signs that something had been dragged, nor did he see any footprints. The small waves from the passing boats would have erased the ones near the water.

A cloud, which had been hiding the sun, drifted east revealing the sun's full brilliance. A reflection of light caught Vernon's attention. He shifted his gaze in the direction of the sparkle, and it glimmered once again.

Sticking up, out of the sand, with the handle jammed into the soft earth was an artist's paint brush.

"Yes! There it is," Vernon said aloud. He laughed and squeezed his fists tight and shook them in victory as he smiled.

Without removing the paint brush from the ground, Vernon studied it. From what little he knew about art, he decided it was about a one inch fan brush. It had a red wooden handle with one notch carved into its surface.

Realizing the killer wanted law enforcement to find this and deciding the killer was keeping track of the deaths with the carved notch, Vernon hurried back to his car and radio.

"Get the crime scene team back over here," Vernon said to Officer Mandelino. He tried to keep the glee out of his voice.

"You find something boss?"

"I did."

"Great. The trucking company you called for just pulled up. Should I tell them they're going to have to wait?"

"I don't think so. The evidence is down near the water and they'll be working up by the site. Send them on. It shouldn't be a problem."

"You got it, boss."

Vernon heard the truck before he saw it. He knew this wasn't in the department's budget, but felt his decision was the right one.

Parking in front of the site, the driver hopped down out of the truck. Vernon waited for men to emerge, but the driver was alone. He was a Hispanic male with a friendly face. The driver saw Vernon and walked toward him with a skip in his step.

Vernon reached for his hand and the two men shook.

"Officer Kearns, I assume?"

"Yes."

"Emilio."

Vernon smiled. The other man's smile was infectious. "If you don't mind me asking, why so cheery?"

"I used to drive a liquid tanker for a big company, and I just started my own. You're my first job. I'm pretty excited to be out on my own."

"Well, that is something to smile about. Congratulations."

"Thank you."

"This job is a little weird," Vernon cautioned.

"I've done weird. One time, my liquid tanker was filled with red water, and I released it over a waterfall at a kid's summer camp. They thought the falls were bleeding."

"That's pretty weird," Vernon said, thinking. "Wasn't that a part of a reality show on television?"

"Yeah, it was."

"Interesting." Vernon described to Emilio what he wanted accomplished and exactly how he wanted it handled. The two men slipped on gloves and Vernon removed the stakes from the tent, depositing the stakes into an evidence bag. With one man on each side, they lifted the tent and carried it to the back of the truck where Emilio had already opened the sliding door.

They slid the tent into the truck. Vernon was surprised at how easily it fit. He had worried it would not. With the tent in the truck, Vernon reminded Emilio of exactly what he wanted to happen at the warehouse. Emilio repeated back to him the instructions, and Vernon was confident it would all be taken care of as he planned.

Vernon watched Emilio pull away and decided to have another look at the strange art on the concrete picnic table as he waited for the crime team. As he turned, an item on the ground underneath the tent had him frozen in place. As the two men had carried the tent to the truck, he had not looked at the ground the tent had hidden. A newspaper sat in the spot where the tent had been.

Vernon crept forward, still tingling from the new revelation. He had read the *Tilley Bee* earlier in the day as he drank his coffee and had his breakfast. From across the camp site he could see the headline, "Murder. Again." The killer had been back since the murder.

Chapter 5

Uncle Karl invited Benny into his studio to talk. Benny thought it would be a strange place, and it was. Hanging on the walls and from the ceiling he saw a green tuba, a polka dotted swordfish, antique saws, dream catchers, scuba gear, and a plethora of other random items. Benny guessed there must have been at least twenty paintings in various stages of completion. Canvases leaned against the walls ten or so deep under handmade signs. Each sign had a symbol which looked to Benny to be Chinese script.

"Did you make those signs?" Benny asked.

"Yes."

"Is that Chinese?"

"Nope."

"Japanese?"

"Nope."

"I give up."

"It's Uncle Karlnese." Uncle Karl walked over to one of the signs that stood above the biggest line of leaning canvases. "This one reads, 'Waste of Time, Get a New Hobby.'" Uncle Karl tried to kick his foot through the first canvas but was unsuccessful. He merely put a giant scuff mark across the painting's surface. He looked at the painting with the new feature and picked it up. His eyes twinkled. "Now we're talking."

Uncle Karl put the painting in a different line of paintings, under a different sign. "This one reads, 'Maybe.'"

"What does the last sign say?" Benny asked, pointing to the last line of paintings.

"It don't *say* anything. Signs can't talk."

"What does it read?"

"It reads, 'Golden,'" Uncle Karl said, making a rainbow motion above his head. "Those are the paintings that keep me going."

"I thought you were a sculptor?"

"I dabble with a little bit of everything."

Uncle Karl pulled the tube of lotion out of his pocket and started to inch closer to Benny. Benny jammed his hands into his pockets and cut him off before he could even ask.

"My hands are beginning to itch. I forgot I'm allergic to aloe," Benny lied.

Uncle Karl took three steps to his left and grabbed a thick rope that hung from the ceiling. He yanked it down and a loud clanging noise filled the air. He repeated the action two more times and stopped. Before the last chime had stopped reverberating in Benny's ears, Angel appeared in the doorway.

Upon seeing nothing was wrong she scolded, "Uncle Karl! The church bell is for emergencies only."

"This is an emergency."

"Mr. James is here, what could be your emergency?"

"He won't rub aloe on my back. Says he's allergic."

"For heaven's sake," she said taking the tube of aloe from her uncle. "Good morning, Mr. James," she said pleasantly, turning and smiling at Benny.

"Good morning."

"Uncle Karl, you have got to stop welding with your shirt off."

"This is the first time this has happened."

"Really?" Angel rubbed lotion into his shoulders with attitude. "Would you like to try that one more time?"

"It's the first time it has happened this month."

"It's the first day of the month! It happened once last month. And, it happened last Thanksgiving. Remember how you missed the meal because you couldn't sit down? I don't even want to think about how it happened."

"I was welding in a strange position behind me and the flap of my pants was blocking my vision."

"I said I don't care." Angel finished rubbing the lotion and handed the tube back to him. She wiped her greasy hands on the back of her jeans and looked at Benny. "I think I'm starting to be allergic to aloe myself." She turned and walked out of the barn.

"Where were we?" Uncle Karl asked.

"You were just about to tell me about the art scene here in Tilley."

"Ah. Chattanooga, Tennessee."

"No. I said Tilley, Georgia."

"But the riff started in Chattanooga. Sit down."

Uncle Karl pointed to a purple bean bag chair behind Benny. It had been a long time since Benny had sat in a bean bag chair, and he slowly lowered himself to the ground and fell into the oddly-shaped thing. Uncle Karl grabbed a wooden rocking horse and pulled it in front of Benny. From a post, he unhooked a cowboy hat, put it on his head, and climbed onto the wooden rocking horse. He began rocking.

"In 1960, I was twenty and full of ideas. Still am. I left the plantation here in search of ideas." Uncle Karl continued rocking and adjusted the cowboy hat atop his head. "This house here was all about money. I wanted something more. Art in the 1960's was evolving as it always does, and I had heard about a group of artists forming in Chattanooga. A bus full of flower-power folks stopped in, heading that way, and one of them let me look at his sketch book. Now, I didn't know one thing about art. I couldn't draw a stick person or dog or pony to save my life. But, I wanted to be a part of what I was seeing. Something about the images in that sketch book set my soul on fire. I wanted to learn how to do that."

Uncle Karl once again pulled the tube of aloe out of his pocket and started rubbing it on his chest and shoulders. As he reached for his back, Benny reluctantly pulled himself out of the bean bag chair and held out his hand for the tube.

"Stop rocking and give me the tube," Benny said.

"I thought you were allergic?"

"I lied. I'm allergic to hairy old white men, but I'll get over it."

Benny filled his hands with aloe and covered Uncle Karl's back with the lotion. As he rubbed, Uncle Karl continued his tale.

37

"When the next flower-power bus came through town, I climbed aboard and went with them. They didn't care that I didn't understand art. They were just happy that I was in love with it. I soon found out that I was actually talented at making sculptures. I could make anything I could touch. It was so easy; I was a natural. And then I tried painting and drawing. I was lost. I failed. My brain didn't think that way. I guess I could say I have a 3-D brain. To make a long story short—I have devoted my life to art. I still make my sculptures with ease, but I live in hopes that one day something in my brain will click and I'll be able to paint and draw the things I see in my mind's eye."

Benny handed the aloe back to Uncle Karl and once again lowered himself into the purple bean bag chair. "This is a fascinating story, don't get me wrong, but what does it have to do with the Tilley art scene?"

"I'm getting there."

Uncle Karl started rocking again.

"In Chattanooga I quickly learned there were two schools of thought when it came to art. There were the new thinkers and the old."

"They were a little behind the times, weren't they? I mean, I'm no art historian, but didn't art take a major turn away from realism and classic ideas in the 1920's?"

"Remember, we're talking about Chattanooga, Tennessee, not New York City."

Uncle Karl pulled the cowboy hat off his head and tossed it to his right without looking. It knocked over a glass jar full of brown water and paint brushes and shattered on the concrete floor. Uncle Karl acted as though he didn't hear it as he didn't turn his head to look and see what happened.

"Switch," Uncle Karl said as he got off the wooden rocking horse.

"You want to sit here?"

"Yeah. And you got to take a ride on this filly."

Uncle Karl fell into the purple bean bag with a sigh. Benny threw his right leg over the wooden horse and settled into the painted saddle.

"If you want the hat, it's over there on the floor. It might be wet and have some glass in it."

"I'll pass." Benny started rocking.

"You ever seen West Side Story?"

"I have."

"The old and new art groups were like the Jets and the Sharks. Two gangs that hated each other."

"The old is always scared of the new," Benny said, "but what does this have to do with Tilley, Georgia?"

Uncle Karl heard something off in the distance and Benny could almost see his ears perk up. Uncle Karl's eyes doubled in size, and he planted his palms down on the concrete floor, ready to pop up out of the bean bag. In the next instant, Benny heard it—the ice cream truck. As Uncle Karl sprinted out the door, Benny checked his watch. It was 9:30 and too early in his mind for an ice cream truck to be making its rounds.

Uncle Karl hopped in place as he waited. Benny walked up beside him and wanted to say something, but somehow he wasn't sure what. As the obnoxious repertoire of songs blaring from the ice cream truck crept closer, Benny finally thought of something to say.

"Really? It's not even ten o'clock in the morning."

"Ice cream is good," Uncle Karl said.

"I've never thought of ice cream as a breakfast food."

"Don't be an old thinker. Join me in new thoughts. What do you pour over cereal?"

"Milk." Benny already knew where this was going.

"What is the main ingredient in ice cream?"

"Milk."

"Thank you! I like my milk frozen."

The truck appeared. It was not an ordinary ice cream truck. A white vehicle approached, which had hundreds of rubber duckies glued to its exterior.

Something clicked in Benny's brain and he asked, "Do you own this truck?"

"Yes! How did you know?"

"I don't know. Maybe the rubber duckies gave it away. Maybe because instead of Yankee Doodle Dandy or Pop Goes the Weasel, the music coming from the truck is unrecognizable noise yet beautiful."

"It's Mozart backwards," Uncle Karl said with a smile.

"Nice touch."

"I make my employee come here first every morning."

"Interesting."

The truck stopped in front of Uncle Karl and Benny. Uncle Karl continued to hop up and down like a child. The driver slid the glass window open and greeted Uncle Karl with cheer.

"Two Super Buddy Chocolate Dips."

"Coming right up, sir."

The man handed Uncle Karl the two ice creams and he gave him money.

"I don't want one of those," Benny said.

"One of them is not for you. But get whatever you like."

"No thanks," Benny said.

Uncle Karl nodded to the driver and he slid the window shut and drove away.

With an ice cream in each hand, Uncle Karl began to eat, going back and forth between cones. It was as if Benny had disappeared. Benny stood and watched in amazement as he devoured the treats like a professional eater. When he was almost finished he popped his head up and walked toward the back of the house. Benny followed.

Clarice, the ostrich was waiting by the fence. Walking over to her, Uncle Karl said, "I didn't forget you." He held out the nearly finished cones and Clarice gobbled both of them.

"Nap time!" Uncle Karl announced.

"What? You haven't finished the story about the art here in Tilley. You actually haven't even started talking about the art in Tilley."

"That's why they make tomorrows." Uncle Karl saluted Benny and said, "Toodles," and disappeared into the house.

Chapter 6

Walking down the dock toward his houseboat, Benny noticed the blinds were now back up in Donny's office. Thoughts of Rachael slipped across his mind and he tried to push them away. Looking toward his boat, he noticed slight movement and knew Vernon was already inside and waiting. Benny had given him a key after a time in which he'd found Vernon camped out on the upper deck of the houseboat one late evening in emotional shambles. It had been a bad day at home and Vernon needed a place to escape to calm his mind. Benny made him a key the next day and told him anytime he needed a place to breath, he was welcome to let himself in and relax.

Benny walked in the door and found Vernon pacing the room. Vernon looked up and smiled.

"That's the smile of a confident man," Benny said, smiling too.

"I think I'm getting good at this."

"You're not getting good; you were already good, and you're just now realizing it."

"Thanks."

"Hungry?" Benny asked.

"Not really, but I know I should eat."

"You should. You talk and I'll cook. You need a drink?"

"No. I'm good."

Benny walked to the fridge and pulled out a spaghetti squash. He turned the oven to 400 degrees. Seemingly at the same time, he pulled out a cutting board and a black frying pan. From the fridge he retrieved a package of lean ground beef and began browning it in the black cast iron pan. With a sizzle in the background he sliced the spaghetti squash in half and scooped out the seeds. He continued to work, drizzling olive oil on the squash as Vernon talked.

"I found some major clues today at the campground."

"Do tell." Benny flipped the squash over on an aluminum foil lined cookie sheet and popped it in the oven. He grabbed two tomatoes and an onion from the fridge.

"I got to really thinking about how the killer got into the campground and decided it had to be by boat."

"Of course. Why didn't we think of that sooner?"

"Don't know. But I found something very interesting down by the water's edge."

"What?" Benny diced the onions and tomatoes and added them to the browned ground beef. He opened a can of tomato paste as he continued listening to Vernon.

"An artist's brush was stuck in the sand with a notch in it!"

"Shut up."

"Not kidding. And that's not it."

"What else?"

"You can tell where the boat landed. They came in hot and heavy. Made a huge gash in the sand."

"I still can't believe I didn't think of the water entrance. I guess I'm a little off today because of Rachael's call last night."

"You doing OK?"

"Yeah. I don't want to talk about it yet."

"All right. Let me know when you do."

"We need to check the boats at all the marinas to see if any of them have muddy spots on their bows."

"Yes. And we need to do that today before they get washed away. I'll get some deputies on it."

Benny opened the oven door slightly to check on the spaghetti squash.

"I don't mean to be rude, but what the hell are you making?"

"Spaghetti."

"Where are the noodles?"

"We are substituting spaghetti squash for noodles."

"Is that what that big yellow thing is?"

"Yes."

"Looks nasty to me. Is this a white thing?"

"No," Benny said laughing. "You'll like it. I was a bit skeptical myself at first. I promise you'll like it."

"You haven't lied to me yet, but I'm thinking we are about to have a first."

"Did you find anything else?"

"I did. I decided to hire a trucking company to move the tent to a warehouse space without breaking it down. I thought it might preserve any evidence inside the tent we may have overlooked."

"Look at you. Damn son! Are you the same guy who was throwing up at the first murder scene we ever worked together?"

"We've been through a lot since then."

"We have."

"When we picked up the tent to put it inside the truck, I found something underneath."

"What?"

"Today's edition of the *Tilley Bee*."

"You've got to be kidding me? The killer went back to the scene?"

"It has to be him," Vernon said.

"Then the gash in the sand could be when he came back."

"I guess it could," Vernon said thinking. "But I would bet my life that the gash is from the first visit to the site. He was nervous and driving fast."

"Wait a minute," Benny said. "What time does the paper get printed?"

"4:20 a.m."

"Yeah. I now remember that from our last case. What time does it go in all those boxes around town?"

"An hour later, I suppose," Vernon said. "I see what you're getting at. Do you think they only made one trip and it was just before dawn? And the newspaper is just supposed to trip us up?"

"That would be my bet," Benny said.

Benny pulled the spaghetti squash out of the oven and shredded it with a large fork. Vernon looked on in horror. Benny took two bowls out and filled each halfway with shredded squash. On top he ladled his homemade marinara. Vernon eyed the dish with skepticism. Sitting at Benny's kitchen table, he slowly brought a forkful to his mouth and chewed. His eyes went from fright to surprise in a moment. He chewed some more and swallowed. Vernon smiled with delight.

"You white folks been keeping this a secret?"

"Yep," Benny said. "That's the way we are."

After lunch, Benny borrowed Donny's speedboat. He had Vernon go over and ask for the keys as he didn't want to get Donny upset again.

Rene also lived on a boat. She lived directly across the lake from the Sleepy Cove Marina. She made her home on a sailboat. Rene came to Tilley a few years back when her husband was transferred from Italy. When he was transferred back, she realized she loved Tilley more than she loved him and she stayed. Her marina was a little bit smaller than Benny's and only catered to sailboats. Of the three marinas on the lake, it was known as the snooty one. It was named X-Sailence. It was against the rules to live on the premises, but Rene somehow talked the owner into it. Benny had often wondered what she had to give up or do to make him budge on the policy.

As Benny steered the boat toward the marina, Vernon made his way to the front of the craft. He gave Benny the thumbs up sign asking him to speed up. Receiving the message, Benny pushed the throttle forward as far as it would go, and the boat skipped across the gentle waters with a rhythmic up and down motion. Vernon held on as the wind rushed across his face.

Nearing the marina, Benny pulled the throttle back.

"That was fun," Vernon said.

"You were acting like you've never been on a boat before."

"I haven't."

"What?"

"I drove a canoe once."

"You don't drive canoes."

"Whatever." Changing topics, Vernon asked, "Do you think Rene even knows anything?"

"No. It's what she doesn't know she knows. You know what I mean?"

"I think I do. Do you know where she parks her boat?"

"Yes. And you don't drive *or* park boats. You dock them in a slip."

"Well, isn't that sophisticated."

"I guess it is." Benny pointed toward a boat and Vernon's eyes followed. "That's it, the one named *Fresh*."

"Do you see what I see?" Vernon asked.

"I do and I'm wondering the same thing you are."

Tied to the side of Rene's boat was a speed boat, pointing outward, with mud covering the bow. Benny eyed the vessel and surmised it was an incredibly expensive boat. The mud on the bow fit exactly what Benny and Vernon were looking for. Benny and Vernon eyed each other as their faces turned solemn.

Benny tied the boat up in one of the slips designated for visitors. He got out of the boat first and steadied it as Vernon jumped from the boat to the dock. Benny wanted to say something but held his tongue as he was glad Vernon didn't end up in the water.

As they neared the row of boats where Rene's was docked, Benny threw his arm out in front of Vernon and pulled him back and out of sight.

"What?" Vernon asked.

"See the boat moving?"

"Yeah."

"Somebody heavy is walking. Maybe they're leaving."

"If we walk up to the front door and knock we can see who is in there with her," Vernon said.

"Yes we can. But if we see them leave on their own and she doesn't tell us they were there, we catch her in a lie."

"What does she have to lie about?"

"That's what we're trying to find out."

"Are you suspicious of everybody?"

"Yep," Benny said. "Even you."

Vernon gave him a look.

"Oh, that's right, you don't know anything about boats. You can't be the person who *drove* the boat and *parked* it on the sand."

"I've created a pretty good alibi for myself, huh?"

"You're a genius."

The sound of a door opening pushed the men back and out of sight. A loud voice echoed through the covered slips, and Benny recognized the voice as the owner of the marina, Big E. He had an unmistakable lazy southern drawl. A moment later,

Big E emerged from the sailboat and laughed. He walked around to the back of Rene's sailboat and boarded his speedboat. He said something else which Benny and Vernon could not quite make out, fired up his boat, and made some waves. Rene went back inside her sailboat and shut the door.

"Let's go," Vernon said.

"No. We don't want her to know we saw him leave. Let's wait a few minutes."

"You seriously think she may have had something to do with this?"

"I don't know, but I learned this lesson the hard way, remember?"

"Oh yeah."

Once upon a time, Benny had been king of the FBI. He'd been investigating a case in which the dean of a prominent university was murdered. A letter opener had been inserted into his heart. Benny was the lead investigator. He put himself in charge of investigating the dean's daughter. As it all turned out, they got involved romantically, and she wound up being the one responsible for the murder. Oops.

"Let's wait five minutes," Benny suggested.

"OK. Do you know Big E personally?"

"I've talked to him a couple of times. He's what I call 'Old Boy Money.'"

"What does that mean?"

"His parents and grandparents owned a lot of the land around the lake before it was a popular place. They sold it a little bit at a time as they needed the cash. As you can imagine, as time went by, the prices climbed. Lakefront property is expensive and they owned almost half of the land that surrounded this lake. When the grandparents died, they passed it on to Big E's parents and as they have aged it seems as though he's inherited the kingdom. He has a brother, but he's in a penitentiary in Colorado. They've sold most of the land beside the marina and the surrounding thirty acres. He's got that in his back pocket if he ever needs some cash, but the rents from the slips bring in major cash, I imagine. How come you don't know him? Seems like he would have needed you at some point"

"His marina is in a different county."

"That's right."

"Can we go now?"

"I'll follow you," Benny said.

Vernon knocked on Rene's door after carefully climbing aboard. She answered with wide eyes.

"Hey guys. You been out there long?"

"No," Vernon said. "We just pulled into the marina as some guy went flying out of here on a speed boat. If I had my radar gun I would've given him a ticket."

Rene laughed. "Did you see who it was?"

"No, I could only tell it was a pretty big guy."

Rene shrugged her shoulders.

Vernon gave Benny a look and Benny tried to hide his amusement.

"Hi Benny," Rene said looking past Vernon. "Why don't you guys come on inside."

Inside, the three settled down in the galley.

"So," Vernon began, "you ready to go back to work?"

"Yeah. It's not like there was a murder in the restaurant itself. Hopefully people will still come to eat and won't be grossed out by the thoughts of the painting made of blood."

"I'll still eat there," Benny stated.

"Me too," Vernon followed. "Can you tell me anything about that day that may have happened differently than most days? Have you thought of who could have done this or had the ability to let somebody in to do this?"

"I opened as usual. I always open. I get there at about six and I always enter through the front door. I don't recall thinking that anything seemed out of order or out of the ordinary. It was just another day. I made a few deserts and prepped stuff for the salads and sandwiches. There weren't any deliveries. The staff arrived at a few minutes before nine. Once I let them inside, I left the front door unlocked. As you know, we don't serve breakfast, but a few people like to stop in and get a cup of coffee."

"Who came in for coffee that morning?" Vernon asked as he pulled out a small notepad.

Rene's eyes looked upward as she searched her brain. "Russell from the Post Office. Jill from the salon next door and one other guy named Kyle who drives a delivery route to Atlanta daily. I pack him a lunch every day as a deal we worked out a year or so ago. And that's it."

"Do you think any of those people would be capable of murdering someone and making a painting out of their blood?"

"No!"

"What about any of your employees?"

"No."

"Then how do you think it could have happened? How could somebody walk through your door with a large canvas and hang it on the wall without anybody noticing?"

"Good question," Rene said. "Believe me, I have been racking my brain trying to figure this out. And I would be lying if I said I wasn't a little bit scared. Why did they pick my restaurant? Does this have anything to do with me or something I've done?"

Vernon looked to Benny who had been quiet on purpose, letting Vernon lead.

"I don't believe so," Benny said shifting in his chair. "You've always been an advocate for the arts and a place where local artists could sell their work. I think your café was just the only place in town that made sense. I don't think it had anything to do with you at all."

"Do you really believe that?"

"Yes, I do." Benny gave her a solemn look. "Do you know a lot of artists in the area."

"Of course. I probably know all of them who sell their work. I must be the only place around where an artist can display and sell their work without paying a dime in commissions."

"Why do you do it?"

"I love art," Rene said with a sly smile. "And it brings in business. The artists want people they know to see their work and they send them here. It's a big deal to have your artwork hanging somewhere. And, most people feel like they have to buy something when they come in since this *is a* restaurant and not an art gallery."

"And once people try your desserts or one of your sandwiches, they're hooked," Vernon said.

"You got it."

"Do you know the Oglethorpe family?" Benny asked.

"Of course I do. Angel works for me."

"Has her mother or uncle ever shown their work at the restaurant?"

"Her mother has. Her uncle is just a crazy old man."

"Do you think he could be the type of person to do something like this?"

"Make a painting out of blood—yes, kill someone—no."

"What kind of work does Angel's mother do?"

"Her name is Nina and she's a mix of Georgia O'Keefe, Jackson Pollack, and Wassily Kandinsky."

"Oh my," Benny said. "So let me get this straight. She paints something in nature, close up, throws sand and other random things in the paint, and has spirit?"

"Have you seen her work?"

"Not yet."

"Show off," Vernon said. "What is she like as a person?"

"Shy, quiet, and withdrawn."

"What do you mean by withdrawn?" Vernon asked.

"I think she's one of those shy people who have a very hard time interacting with people, even in the simplest exchanges. She only brought her work here because there was such a bad leak in her roof. If she didn't need the money she never would have come."

"And people bought her work?" Vernon asked.

"Yes."

"Can I finish this story?" Benny asked.

"Be my guest," Rene said smiling.

"You bought her work."

"I did."

"You're good people," Vernon said.

"Would you like a painting of a maple leaf, which has pieces of pine straw in it, and every color you ever imagined? I don't have room for a lot of paintings here on the sailboat."

Benny and Vernon laughed and gave each other a secretive nod. They stood in unison.

"We'll let you get back to whatever you were doing," Vernon said. "We just wanted to check on you and ask a few questions. Let me know if you think of anything else."

"I will."

Benny pretended to sniff the air when he told Rene goodbye and had eye contact with her.

"Do you smell gas or something?" Rene asked.

"No, I just caught a whiff of a man's cologne. You must have had a guest earlier."

54

"No. You two are the only people who've come over today."

"Maybe it's my new deodorant," Benny said. "The store was out of my usual."

As Rene turned to walk to the door, Vernon shot Benny a look and Benny stuck his tongue out at him.

Chapter 7

Benny steered the boat back toward his marina. When they were out of earshot from Rene's, Vernon busted out laughing. Benny pulled the throttle back and slowed the boat.

"Would you like to share?" Benny asked.

"Did you really smell cologne? I didn't smell anything."

"No. I didn't smell anything either, but I wanted her to lie to my face."

"Why?"

"Because I've studied lies. Faces do different things with different types of lies and I wanted to read her face."

"And?"

"It was definitely an ashamed lie."

"Ashamed of what?"

"My guess is she's sleeping with Big E so he'll let her live at the marina. That's all. Just a guess."

"Why wouldn't she just get an apartment or a house?"

"I imagine she likes living on her boat. Who knows why people do the things they do."

"How about I check Big E out this afternoon, and you see if you can have a chat with Nina Oglethorpe."

"Sounds good. We need a photo of the front of Big E's boat. Do you think one of your deputies can find it and snap one?"

"I'll do it."

"Really? Are you going to *drive* a canoe around the lake and look for his boat? And if you find it, you'll *park* your canoe and take a couple of photos?"

"Have I told you lately that you're hilarious?"

"No, you haven't."

"I wonder why?"

Benny laughed and pushed the throttle down as Vernon chuckled and settled into his seat.

Vernon spotted Big E's boat at the Sleepy Cove Marina. Benny slowed the boat.

"That was easy," he told Benny. "I have a little point and shoot camera in the car."

As Benny tied the boat, he noticed Big E walking out of Donny's office toward his boat.

"Hurry and get the camera. I'll try to make small talk with him."

Vernon hurried up the dock and Big E yelled to Donny that he would get him next time. Benny heard his southern drawl and wondered how much he weighed. He guessed he was pushing 350 or more.

"Afternoon," Benny said approaching Big E.

"Afternoon," he responded without making eye contact. He tried to step past Benny. Benny stood his ground in the middle of the narrow dock.

"Can I help you?"

"You don't remember me?" Benny tried.

"You think everybody should remember you because you used to be some hotshot FBI agent and you've been on TV a few times?"

"No. We've met twice. That is why you should remember me."

"Oh," Big E said with a sigh. "So we have. How do you do Mr. James?"

"Call me Benny, Mr. Frederick."

"My father is Mr. Frederick. I'm Ernest, but prefer Big E."

"I did remember but didn't want to assume I could call you that."

"Is there something you needed to speak to me about? I don't mean to be rude, but I'm in a bit of a hurry."

Big E looked over his shoulder to see Vernon approaching.

"Is that the cop under Chief Neighbors?"

"Yes."

"Is he coming to talk to me?"

Benny could tell he was becoming very nervous and wasn't sure how to play his hand. Benny nodded his head slowly.

"Oh Jesus," Big E said. "I knew it was wrong and I knew it was illegal, but I didn't think that anybody really cared.

"Why wouldn't anybody care?" Benny said as Vernon arrived next to the two men.

"It's just not a big deal," Big E said.

Benny lifted his eyebrows to Vernon signaling he wasn't sure what was going on.

"So you don't think it's a big deal?" Vernon said. "Are you crazy?"

"It's only a hundred dollars!" Big E said.

Now Benny and Vernon had no idea what Big E was talking about.

"And?" Vernon questioned, not sure what he was questioning.

"And gambling with a bookie in Georgia is wrong."

Benny's and Vernon's eyes shot open wide with understanding.

"You're damn right it is," Benny said. "Vernon, can I please have a word with this man alone?" Benny pointed his thumb toward Big E's boat and Vernon hustled over to snap some photos.

Benny grabbed Big E's chunky arm and wheeled him around to where his back was to Vernon.

"His dad lost all their family's money one time growing up because of gambling," Benny said beginning his lie. "Vernon just sniffed out this little thing going on here and he's all bent out of shape about it. Let me see if he'll let you slide on this one, but you'll owe me one, OK?"

"Anything," Big E said with fervent nod.

Benny had noticed Vernon was finished taking photos and walked down the dock to him.

Benny looked Vernon in the eyes. "Just walk past him in a huff and tell him he owes me one. I'll explain later."

"You have got to be kidding me," Vernon said huffing up the dock and playing along. He stopped in front of Big E. "You owe that man a big one. He just did you a big favor."

"I do. I sure do."

Vernon walked past him and yelled back, "Get out of my county."

As Big E disappeared, Benny and Vernon had another good laugh as Benny explained to Vernon what had just happened.

As Vernon headed back to the police department, Benny drove back toward the Oglethorpe place. He tried to get Vernon to come along without any luck. Driving through town, Benny had an idea of how he could keep Uncle Karl busy so he could have some time alone with Nina.

Pulling into Red's driveway, he spotted him in his garden as usual. Hearing the Jeep, Red jerked his head and a giant smile streaked across his face.

"Bendy!" he called, running toward the Jeep. Benny quickly got out. "You come and make a visit on Red."

"I did. I was about to head out to the Oglethorpe place and wondered if you wanted to ride along."

"Red not knowing the Ogerthorpe's."

"It's Oglethorpe's," Benny corrected. "Uncle Karl's last name is Oglethorpe."

Red's face lit up. "I going! Let Red get a bag of yummy tomatoes for he."

"OK. No rush, Red. Can I use your bathroom?"

"Bendy can be doing anything he like."

"Thanks, buddy."

Benny had not been inside the house in a while. He and Red usually talked in the yard by the garden or on the front porch. He entered through the front door and stopped. Paintings covered the walls.

"Red!" Benny called.

"You not liking?" Red asked rushing through the front door.

"Where did you get these?"

"Red make."

"You made these?"

"Yep. Red make."

"How did you make these?" Benny could not believe Red had made the paintings, but had never known Red to lie before.

"Red using paint and brushes."

"That's not what I meant. How do you know how to paint?"

"You just put you little brush in paint and put all you colors on you picture."

Benny looked at the paintings and at Red. He looked back and forth with wonder. The paintings were of vegetables, gardens and sunlight lifting vegetation into the sky.

"How?" was all Benny could muster.

"Red just look at he garden and paint what he see. It easy, Bendy. Art bees easy."

"You amaze me Red. You never cease to amaze me."

"You maze me, Bendy. Red be making you a painting but it not be ready."

"I can't wait," Benny said finally, leaving the room and making his way to the bathroom.

In the Jeep on the way to the Oglethorpe place, Benny told Red how he wished to have a few minutes alone with Nina. As far as Benny could tell, Red understood his job was to keep Uncle Karl in the studio and out of their way.

Uncle Karl peeked his head out of the studio as he heard the gravel crunching under the vehicle's tires. It wasn't hard for him to notice Red as he had the window down waving. Uncle Karl's serious look brightened.

"I bring you some tomatoes," Red said exiting the car and handing Uncle Karl the brown paper sack. "Red owing you only 976 more."

Uncle Karl opened the crumpled sack and peered inside. "How do you do it Red?"

"Tomato can be hard and Red promise he Mama he never tell the secret of world's best tomato."

"You can tell your Uncle Karl."

"You not Red real uncle." Uncle Karl's face fell, and Red recognized his disappointment. "I sorry Uncle Karl. From now on in Red brain, you Red real uncle." Uncle Karl's face returned to happy. "Now show Red you new paintings."

"Follow me."

Uncle Karl never acknowledged Benny or looked in his direction. He laughed to himself and walked to the front door. The doorbell hung from a suspicious looking wire. Benny was sure plantation houses did not have wired doorbells and wondered when it had been installed. Whenever it had, it was obvious by the condition of it that it had been a long time.

Benny doubted the doorbell worked but pulled the hanging wires and the device up to himself anyway. He noticed a dull orange glow behind the button and pushed. As he pushed the button, he stood still and listened but did not hear if it actually worked or not. As he tried to decide if he should push the button again or knock, he heard footsteps approaching.

Angel pulled the massive door open. "Hi."

"How are you?"

"I'm fine. Uncle Karl is in his studio."

"I saw him. I'm actually here to see your mother. Is she home?"

"Uh, yeah. She never leaves."

"Oh," was all Benny could think to say remembering how Rene had characterized her.

"And, she doesn't like visitors, or people to be quite honest. Probably why she never leaves."

"It's important. Will you ask her for me?"

"OK. She'll say no."

"Tell her it's the cops and if she doesn't come speak to me, I will come to her."

"You would do that?"

"No. Just give it a shot."

"I'll give it a shot."

Angel disappeared into the house and Benny took in the room. He marveled at the high ceilings and wood floors. The paint peeling from the walls almost looked intentional as it made an incredible texture. The pieces were long and mostly curled. Pieces that had fallen were sprinkled around the floor. A broom and dust pan stood in a corner. Benny wondered if the house was safe to inhabit. Listening for footsteps and not hearing any, he crept forward and looked into the next room. It happened to be the dining room. A white sheet covered a giant table. Benny lifted a corner and peered underneath. He saw what he figured to be the original antique table, set for at least a dozen or more with dishes he imagined were nearly priceless. Giant oil paintings adorned the walls and a stunning chandelier hung from the ceiling. The chandelier was dusty and littered with paint peelings. Benny heard footsteps and hurried back to the foyer.

Angel emerged smiling. "She said she will see you in her studio."

"Wow. Did you have to threaten her?"

"No. I told her you were handsome. She has a soft spot for handsome men."

Benny blushed. Angel turned and he followed her down the hall. At the end of the hall was a set of double doors and before she opened them, Angel paused and turned around.

"This is where it gets really ugly," she said solemnly. "The front of the house is bad, but reality sets in right here."

Angel pushed the double doors open and the house changed. The walls that were peeling on the one side were now brown and damp. The serviceable wood floors from the front suddenly transformed to cracked, splintered, and uneven wood. Benny spotted at least a half-dozen five-gallon buckets placed strategically throughout the hallway to catch drops of rain.

Angel noticed his face. "Told you. Mom's studio is at the back of the house. Watch where you step."

Benny followed Angel down the ominous hall and wondered what it looked like behind the closed doors along the way. He almost stopped Angel to ask her if he could take a look at one of the rooms but decided it would be rude. At the end of the hall was an out of place, blindingly white door in which light poured from underneath.

"This is where the magic happens," Angel said. With that, she turned and walked away.

Benny watched her vanish. He lightly tapped on the door thinking Nina must certainly know he had arrived. He listened for footsteps and didn't hear any. Still silent, the light coming from under the door changed and Benny could tell there was movement.

Nina slowly pulled the door open and looked Benny in the eyes. Light radiated from behind her body and Benny stood still, speechless, lost in her softness and blue eyes. Nina smiled but still did not speak. She waved her hand for Benny to come inside and he followed, still without words.

The room was the brightest place Benny had ever been inside. It seemed as though everything in the room was warm, vibrating, and radiant. He watched Nina walk across the room and turn to face him. Light glimmered from her hair. Her cheeks were soft and delicate. Benny wondered when they had last seen the sun. As Benny studied her, the word "soft" kept floating across his brain. Her hair seemed soft, as well as her skin. Her body was not petite or big, but soft. Her clothes were soft. Her stare was soft, and so was her smile.

"Forgive the disastrous state of my home." Her voice—soft.

"Shit happens." Benny could not believe the words that had just come out of his mouth. "I mean, it's nothing to be ashamed of. This type of thing takes more than one generation to happen. Why don't we blame the last and leave it at that?"

"Let's," Nina answered. "I hear you have met Karl?"

"I call him Uncle Karl for some reason and yes, we've met."

"He's not well."

"You don't say?"

"Are you mocking me?"

"No," Benny answered, although he was.

"He may seem lucid and just a bit off, but he is on some very powerful medications. Sometimes he forgets to take some of them."

"I did see him talking to an ostrich. And he eats ice cream for breakfast every day."

"Did he tell you he owns the company?" Nina asked softly.

"Yes, he did tell me that."

"He doesn't. That's one of his lies."

"But." Benny thought of the rubber duckies glued to the ice cream truck and the backwards music. "But it was all so strange like his personality. I thought he had to be the one to create it?"

"He reflects."

"He does what?"

"He reflects the personalities he is consumed with at the time. He is always different. If you talk to him long enough, he will start to sound like you. Have you noticed it?"

"I haven't."

"He hasn't known you long enough then. After three exposures to you—he will be able to mimic you perfectly."

"No way."

"Just wait."

"Is he dangerous?"

"Only if he sees dangerous. It's one of the reasons we don't have television. Besides all of the other obvious reasons." Nina laughed softly.

"What about the art?" Benny asked.

"He's never made a piece of art in his life."

Benny blanked.

Nina laughed.

"You don't get shocked often, Mr. James. It's quite cute."

Nina blushed and began fiddling with some of her art supplies.

"Then who made it all?"

"I did."

Benny's face turned white.

"Even the sculptures?" Benny asked.

"Yes. Even the sculptures." Nina studied an unmarked jar that sat among another dozen or so other unmarked jars and unscrewed the lid. A fan behind her pushed the air toward Benny.

Benny thought the lights were getting brighter and he wondered how that could happen when they were already the brightest lights he had ever seen. Blood bubbled up from his toes to his head and swirled. Benny fainted.

Chapter 8

Chief Neighbors had a mirror inside his desk drawer. He pulled the drawer open and checked himself. He closed it and picked up the phone. He had a redhead and an urgent call waiting.

"You had better get your boy in check," Big E said.

"Come again, my boy?" Chief Neighbors did not have too much going for him morally, but he *was* protective of his officers.

"You heard me, Charles. Your boy is out of line," Big E repeated.

"I'll speak to him," Chief Neighbors said, slumping down in his chair. Although Big E's marina was in a different county, they shared the same lake and Big E didn't like owning only half of anything. He gave generously to Chief Neighbors' reelection campaign every four years.

"You'd better," Big E said, hanging up the phone.

Chief Neighbors stood and began pacing his office.

Big E began pacing his as well. His office overlooked the lake with a picture perfect view. The lake house sat atop a steep slope. Big E sometimes thought of himself as a King looking down on his kingdom as he peered across the waters. Not being one who cared to exercise or exert too much energy, Big E had paid big bucks for a paving company to construct a wide sidewalk so he could drive a golf cart up and down to get to and from the dock and his boats.

The office was converted from a home he bought dirt cheap in foreclosure. He turned the spacious great room into a boardroom of sorts, including a large conference table to one side, which had seldom been used. Big E had gutted two of the bedrooms to make the great room even larger. With the help of an interior designer and some talented carpenters, the room rivaled New York city's finest office spaces.

Although Big E was not an art aficionado, he collected pieces, as he saw art as a sign of wealth. Expensive paintings graced the walls and eclectic sculptures were thoughtfully placed throughout the room. He rarely studied the paintings as they meant very little to him. One of the paintings did pique his curiosity and he found himself lost in it more and more. Something about it tugged at his mind. It was painted by a local artist—Nina Oglethorpe.

Chief Neighbors summoned Vernon and Benny to his office. They arrived separately, but at the same time.

"What's this about?" Benny asked as the two men neared the front door.

"I don't know, but he was pissed."

The tiny police department was empty. Chief Neighbors' office door was closed. Vernon knocked. And waited.

A full minute later the door opened. A redhead in sunglasses walked out with her head pointed toward the floor. Her hair and clothes were tousled.

Vernon smirked. Benny chuckled. They walked into the office.

"Afternoon meeting?" Benny asked.

"Yes," Chief Neighbors said, trying to tuck his shirt into his pants as he was still seated behind his desk. With his shirt tucked, he pulled at his mustache and tried to be serious. "She is the new, um, the new..."

"The new piece of ass?" Benny asked.

Chief Neighbors' face lit up like Christmas. "Yes! And she's a devil in sheep's clothing. You wouldn't believe the tricks that gal can do. My goodness!"

"You've got lipstick on your face, Chief," Vernon said, pointing to the right side of his own face.

Chief Neighbors pulled open the desk drawer containing his mirror and wiped away the evidence of his fling.

"You boys are lucky," he said closing the drawer.

"Why is that?" Vernon asked.

"Well, before the redheaded gal showed up I was absolutely furious with you two. Now I am only slightly perturbed."

"Can I get her number for the next time we piss you off?" Benny joked.

"I put her on my speed dial," the Chief answered, completely missing the attempt at humor.

"What were you mad about?" Vernon probed.

"I got a call a few hours ago from across the lake."

"Oh," Vernon said, clueing in. "Big E."

"Yes. Big E called and yelled at me." Chief Neighbors pouted. "He was *irate*."

"Why do you care?" Benny asked. "He's not one of your constituents, so to speak."

"He seems to think he was being harassed in my county and I...," Chief Neighbors searched for a lie.

"And he has a lot of money," Vernon said.

"He's loaded," answered the Chief.

"And you don't want to lose one of the biggest contributors to your re-election fund," Benny guessed.

Chief Neighbors pulled at his mustache. "No." He pulled some more.

"You're a terrible liar," Benny said.

"How do you know that? Those were secret donations."

"Aren't those illegal?"

"Not if they remain secret," Chief Neighbors shot back. "We're getting off the point here. I have my reasons for doing the things I do and this county is better for it."

"I'll never tell," Benny said.

"Do tell how you knew," Chief Neighbors pleaded.

"I've been around the block, Charles. I read signs and I make educated guesses."

"So now you're psychic?"

"Just intuitive. Would you like to tell us why Big E was so angry?"

"I was hoping you would tell me," Chief Neighbors admitted.

"You tell him," Benny said to Vernon.

"We caught him doing some illegal gambling."

"In Donny's pool?"

"You know about that, Chief?"

"I... I... just discovered it." Chief Neighbors pulled at his mustache.

"You know we have his books," Benny bluffed.

"Did he put my real name in those books?" Chief Neighbors yelled. He stood up and pounded his fist on the desk. "That dumb redneck!"

"Charles, Charles," Benny calmed. "No. Stop talking. Should I call the redhead back? Everything is fine. We don't know anything about anything," Benny lied. "We'll leave Big E alone. To us, he doesn't exist. Happy?"

"Nothing said here gets out of this room," Chief Neighbors stated.

"Nothing," Vernon said.

"Nothing," Benny echoed.

As Vernon and Benny walked out of his office, Chief Neighbors was punching the speed dial on his phone.

In the parking lot, Benny and Vernon decided to go to Rene's for a drink. They heard she had reopened earlier and besides wanting a drink, they were both curious to see if it was business as usual at the café.

They walked in the restaurant to find a few customers scattered about the room. It was mid-day and usually a slow time. Benny picked his and Vernon's favorite spot by the front window and sat down. After sitting, they spotted Angel emerging from the kitchen. As she eyed them her mouth widened into a devilish grin.

"Whatever she says is a lie," Benny quickly said to Vernon.

Vernon shot him a confused look. "What?"

"Hello officers," Angel said in a singsong voice.

Benny nodded and Vernon asked, "What's with the evil smile?"

"Mr. James didn't tell you?"

"Mr. James doesn't give away his secrets easily."

Angel looked at Benny playfully and raised her eyebrows.

"OK," Benny said. "I'll spill. When I met Angel's mother I fainted for the first time in my life. It was hot and bright and my senses were overwhelmed by some sort of rancid chemicals she had in a jar."

Vernon bent over in a fit of laughter. "The great FBI man faints. I'll be damned."

"It was much less of a faint than a loss of my senses for a few moments."

"My mother said you were lying prostrate on the floor. I think she even said something about drool."

"She did not!"

"I made that part up," Angel admitted. "She did say you were awfully cute, though."

"She did not."

"Yeah, she really did. You should call her."

Benny was not used to blushing, but he did.

"What can I get you guys?" Angel asked, changing the subject.

"Two Buds."

"Two beers coming up." Angel walked away from the table.

"Don't you dare say anything," Benny warned.

"About what? The fainting or Angel's mom having the hots for you?"

"Neither."

"What's she look like?"

"Don't want to talk about it."

"It might help you forget Rachael." Benny gave him a look. "OK. Let's change the subject."

"Thanks."

"I was able to rustle up a good picture of our first victim," Vernon said. He pulled the photo out of his pocket and showed it to Benny.

"That looks like him all right, minus all the slashes I last saw him with. What do you know about him?"

"He's not from around here. I'm still working on the rest."

"Let me know when you uncover some more."

"So, how are we going to put the screws to Big E without the Chief knowing about it?"

"We'll have to be sneaky. We'll have to lie to him about what we're doing, and we'll also have to make sure Big E doesn't see us snooping around him or find out we're checking him out."

"Why do you think he had mud on the front of his boat?"

"Good question," Benny said rubbing his chin.

Angel arrived with two Budweiser bottles, set them on the table, and scurried off without a word.

"I can't picture Big E hopping out of a boat on one of the islands, can you?" Vernon asked.

"I can't imagine his fat ass hopping at all."

"Maybe it's not his boat," Vernon suggested.

"Let's find out. When you took the photo, did you get the identification number on the side of the boat?"

"Yep."

"Run it when you get back to the office and we'll go from there."

As both men were about to touch their bottles to their lips, Vernon's cell phone rang and they both paused.

"Officer Kearns," he said and listened. "Dammit. On my way," he said standing.

Benny stood as well. "What?"

"More bloody art."

"Where?"

"The Police Department."

Chapter 9

Tilley's Police Department was the size of a gas station—a small one. It had an office for Chief Neighbors, an oversized closet used as an interrogation room, another closet-sized room to store property, and one more small area with a long counter that separated a few desks and a waiting area.

On top of the counter sat a welded compilation of rusted auto parts. The sculpture looked like a candle holder, but instead of a candle there was a finger. A single, bloody finger.

"Chief!" Vernon yelled.

"I'm in here," Chief Neighbors yelled from behind his office door.

Vernon walked into his office and as usual, whenever anything involving blood happened, Chief Neighbors was pale and nursing a Sprite.

"Don't say it," Chief Neighbors said looking at Benny.

"Why did you get into this line of work?" Benny asked.

"This kind of thing is not supposed to happen here," the Chief tried.

"You should have been anything else," Benny snapped.

"Just tell us what happened," Vernon said.

"I was really upset after you guys left and I called an old friend to come down and comfort me. She calmed me down, and when she went to leave and walked out the door I heard her scream. I ran to the door and saw the candle thing and called you guys."

"Where's Officer Mandelino?" Vernon asked.

"He's off doing some things you asked him, I believe."

"And you didn't hear anything?" Benny asked. "Isn't there a bell on the front door you can hear if your office door is closed?"

"Yes," Chief Neighbors answered.

"Did you hear it go off a few minutes ago?"

"Yes."

"And?" Benny asked.

"I figured it was one of you guys. And I was busy being comforted."

"Oh for Chrissake," Benny said. "Did you hear anything out of the ordinary?"

Chief Neighbors just looked at Benny. Benny's face turned red and his brain started to spin. He knew he should not say what he was thinking, but his anger trumped his common sense and he screamed, "How in the hell do you win re-election every four years? You are an incompetent boob and Vernon could do your job with both of his eyes closed and his hands tied behind his back."

"I don't want your job, boss," Vernon tried. Vernon looked at Benny and shook his head trying to tell him to cool it.

Benny caught the communication and took a few deep breaths. "I'm sorry, Chief. I know you can't forget what I said, but I would like to take it back. This is just pissing me off. I came to Tilley to retire and get away from all of this madness, and it just seems to follow me around."

"Why don't we all just forget our personal differences and try to solve this case," Vernon suggested.

"Great idea," Benny said.

"I agree," Chief Neighbors said.

"So," Vernon started, "we have another sick piece of art we're supposed to figure out. Who has any ideas?"

The men all stared at the rusted sculpture holding the finger.

"It's made out of auto parts," Chief Neighbors said holding his hand in front of his face like he was shielding the sun from his eyes.

"What are you doing?" Benny asked.

"If I hold my hand like this, I can't see the bloody finger and I won't throw up."

"We should put that on your re-election posters," Benny said.

"Benny!" Vernon cautioned.

"Sorry," Benny said. "Great technique, Chief."

"Can we just assume there is a dead body that goes with this finger?" Vernon asked Benny.

"Definitely. Does it look like a man's or a woman's finger?"

Chief Neighbors held his mouth and ran into his office slamming the door behind him.

"You upset him on purpose," Vernon said.

"Please don't take up for him. Let's get a closer look at this," Benny said inching closer. "Tell me what you see," he instructed.

"OK." Vernon took a closer look. "I can tell by the discolored skin that the finger was removed from the body at least 24 hours ago."

"Good," Benny said nodding his head with approval. "What about the blood dripping down and around the finger?"

"It must have been added recently. It definitely did not come from this finger as the tissue looks dried. It seems to be a poor attempt to fool whoever they thought would find this into thinking this just happened. I would guess this happened yesterday or the day before and someone was just waiting for the right time to place this for us to find."

"Good. I agree with everything you've said. Make sure we find out if the blood dripping over and around the finger matches the blood type inside the finger. I suspect it does, but if it doesn't, we might have another new problem."

"So where's our clue?" Vernon asked. "How does this lead us to a body?"

"I don't know."

"Isn't that what our killer wants? He wants us to find a body from this clue?"

"I think so. So, let's look at his pattern so far—even though it is only one murder, I always assume there's a pattern. What's the pattern?"

"In the last murder he used numbers. He used the number four in the painting, and the body was found on site number four of the Talking Pines Campground."

"So, if we are going by that thesis, what number do we have here?"

Vernon looked at the finger sticking into the air and it hit him. "Number one!"

"I think so," Benny agreed. "I don't think he would use the campground again, but we might as well check there first."

"I believe site number one is actually visible from the check-in station, so I highly doubt the body will be there, but I'll send a deputy by to check it out."

"What else has the number one attached to it around here?"

"Well, none of the roads do besides the mile markers."

"Put that on the list for the deputies to check."

"Is there an address in town you can think of that has a one in it that might stand out?"

"No. I think everything starts at one hundred and goes up from there. The slips at your marina are numbered, aren't they?"

Benny's face fell. "I'm number one."

"I think you would have noticed a dead body when you left this morning."

"This nasty bastard could have moved it to my boat since then."

"I didn't get the feeling that this was anything personal against you, did you?"

"No, but I *have* put a lot of people in prison and somebody could be looking for revenge."

"Possible," Vernon said. "I just don't get that feeling. Why don't you go check it out real quick while I take care of this crime scene."

"That would make me feel better."

"On your way back, will you swing by the One Stop and pick up a Dr. Pepper for me?"

Benny was already headed for the door and jerked his head back.

"That's it!"

"What?"

"Think about what you just said."

Vernon thought. "The One Stop!"

"It has to be. Think about the sign."

"You're right. It has a hand with one finger pointing in the air next to the words."

As Benny ran out the door, Vernon called, "I still want a Dr. Pepper!"

The One Stop was a fairly seedy establishment with a revolving door of employees. It had all your gas station essentials plus a few extras. Benny felt certain the slot machines in the back room were illegal. He also marveled at the wide selection of adult magazines offered behind the counter and the glass case displaying water bongs and pipes in plain view accompanied by a sign that read, "For Tobacco Use Only." The inside of the station always smelled like cigarette smoke and incense.

Unfortunately for Benny, it was the closest store to the Sleepy Cove Marina and sometimes out of necessity he had to stop in and buy something. The employees always gave him the creeps, and he oftentimes wondered where the owner found them. The average employee lasted about four months before they quit because of burnout and the long hours or were fired for stealing or some other impropriety.

Benny entered the store to find a new face behind the counter, and he immediately sized him up as an alcoholic or drug user. The clerk was an older man with wispy gray hair and a beard which had not been cut or trimmed in quite some time. He had the look of someone who didn't want to look completely disheveled, but still did. As Benny neared he smelled strong body odor mixed with stale cigarette smoke and cheap cologne. Benny gave him his best fake smile. When the clerk returned it with a fake one of his own he spotted a mouth full of yellow and at least two missing teeth.

"How you doing this afternoon?" Benny asked.

The clerk coughed up some phlegm and cleared his throat as he muttered, "Hanging."

"Hanging," Benny repeated. "Like hanging in there?"

"Yeah. You being smart with me?"

"No. I just wasn't too sure what you meant."

"What do you need?"

"I need to take a look around," Benny said watching his eyes.

"What are you looking for?"

"I'll know it when I see it."

The clerk's eyes twitched, and he studied Benny as if he had just woken up from a deep sleep.

"Well, look on then," he said as his hands started to fidget. He scratched his face nervously and pulled a pack of Camel's out of his dirty shirt pocket. With a trembling hand he put one in his mouth and lit it.

"I've been around the block a time or two," the clerk told Benny.

"I can tell."

"And I can tell you're the law."

Benny flashed him his credentials.

"Oh, Jesus."

"Calm down," Benny said holding out his hand.

"I don't know anything about the video slots and poker machines in the back. If the customers win, they have to come back when the boss is here for the payout. I swear. And the pipes and bongs, I know people buy them to smoke grass, but there's nothing I can do about it."

"I'm not here about anything like that. I just want to ask you a few questions."

"OK."

"How long have you worked here?"

"Not even a week, man."

"How many days?"

"Five."

"Have you noticed anything strange or out of the ordinary?"

"Oh yeah."

"What?"

"This guy came in this morning at 6:30 and bought coffee, Crisco, and a copy of Super Jugs," he said pointing over his shoulder to the adult magazines behind him.

"That is a little strange," Benny agreed. Anything else?"

"Yeah," the clerk said stubbing out his cigarette and lighting another one. "A girl came in yesterday and bought a whole roll of lottery tickets and paid with all one dollar bills. She also bought a lollipop. Green."

Benny nodded his head. "Again, strange, but not exactly what I was looking for."

"I can go on for days and I have only worked here for six days."

"I thought you said five days before?"

"Yeah. Five. They all run together, man."

"Is it OK if I look around now? You're not in any trouble. I'm working on a case that has nothing to do with the day to day operations of this gas station. I just think the person I'm looking for might have come by here and left something."

"Why didn't you just say that man?"

"I don't know," Benny answered. "I don't know."

Benny turned and walked toward the soda cooler to get Vernon's Dr. Pepper before he forgot. As he neared the cooler, the room opened up and a soda display filled the open area. Twelve-packs of soda were stacked at least six feet high in a rainbow shape around the biggest cooler Benny had ever seen. Taped to the wall of twelve pack containers was a handwritten sign that read, "It's the One."

Benny's heart began racing. "What's this?" he yelled to the front of the store. "Get back here!"

The clerk hustled to the back with a cigarette flapping between his lips.

"It's a soda display, man."

"What's with the slogan and the giant cooler?"

"You drink it and it cools you down. That's what the commercials say. Don't you watch television man?"

"Not much," Benny admitted.

"I guess there's a contest to win the cooler or something. I don't really know anything about that," the clerk said.

"Did you see the person who set this up?"

"Yeah, man. Some fat guy. He had a real hard time. I thought he was going to pass out and die here on the floor. He was sweating like a whore in church."

"Nice," Benny said. "Have you ever seen a cooler this big?"

"No. Kind of ridiculous if you ask me."

"Mind if I look inside?"

"Be my guest."

Benny held his breath and lifted the top of the cooler. As he suspected, inside was a body, minus a finger, curled in the fetal position. Ice covered the body and had melted to a thin layer revealing the contents underneath.

"Jesus Christ!" the clerk screamed as he tripped backwards and fell on his back. "I... I..." He began shaking and pulled himself off the floor and sprinted to one of the coolers containing beer and cheap wine. He opened the cooler door and yanked out a bottle of Night Train, unscrewed the top, and drank the entire bottle in one tilt.

Benny watched in amazement. "Feel better?" he asked when the clerk lowered the bottle.

"I will in a minute. Maybe I'll sip on one more while we wait for the cops."

"Good idea." Benny pulled his cell phone out of his pocket and called Vernon. Vernon answered on the first ring. "I've got your Dr. Pepper here and a dead body."

"My God. All right. The guys are almost finished taking pictures here and collecting. I'll tell them to head on over when they're finished here. I think they can wrap the rest up without me and I'll be right over."

"I'll put your soda back in so it'll be cold for you."

"Thanks."

Vernon breezed through the door less than ten minutes later and rushed to the back of the station. He stopped in front of the opened cooler and peered inside.

"What the hell is going on?"

"It's a game. Somebody's messing with us."

"Why?"

Benny shrugged his shoulders.

"Is the guy sipping on the bottle of Night Train the clerk?"

"Yeah." Benny got Vernon up to speed on the situation.

Vernon shook his head and called the clerk over. "I still have the picture of our first vic," he said to Benny as he pulled the photo out of his breast pocket.

The clerk put the finishing touches on the second bottle of Night Train and wiped his mouth. Vernon held the picture of victim number one in front of his face.

"Ever seen this guy?"

"That's the guy who delivered all the twelve-packs and set up the display with the cooler."

"Thanks," Vernon said putting the picture away. "Why don't you take a couple more of those bottles home with you since you seem to like them so much and we'll come see you tomorrow for a formal statement."

"Like free?"

"Free. Just leave me your address and phone number."

"OK. But I don't have a phone number."

"No problem. Just the address will be fine."

The clerked scuttled off.

"So," Vernon said turning his focus back on Benny, "the fat guy delivers a dead body in a cooler to the gas station and then gets offed. Who's behind this?"

"I would think somebody put him up to it."

"Do you think he knew what was in the cooler?"

"I'm thinking he did." Vernon looked at the cooler. "It doesn't have a lock on it or anything to keep it sealed. Any normal person would look inside to see why it was so heavy. Natural instinct."

"Maybe the ice completely covered the body when it was delivered."

"Could be."

"Or, the fat guy killed the guy in the cooler and then somebody killed him."

"No, I don't get that feeling. Do you? Back in the day, did you ever work off a feeling?"

"Yeah, I worked off feelings and then I tried to back those feelings up with facts. If your facts don't match your feelings—you know something is wrong. And yes, I get the feeling that we're just going to be looking for one killer."

"What do you know about the fat guy? What would motivate him to do somebody's dirty work like this. Money? A woman?"

"I'm gonna have to go with a woman on this one. Dumping a body inside a gas station among a display of twelve-packs is crazy. Money can make people do some crazy things, but this is woman crazy thinking right here."

"I agree. The crew is here," Vernon said glancing over his shoulder at the noise behind him.

"Speaking of women, I'm going to head on over and talk to Nina Oglethorpe. I want to ask her permission to talk to Uncle Karl's doctor. I still need to rule him out in case what we're dealing with here is not caused by woman-crazy or money-crazy but just crazy-crazy."

Chapter 10

Nina was sitting on her front porch. Benny was thankful he didn't have to go back into her studio again. She recognized his Jeep coming down the drive and began combing her hair with her fingers. She quickly stood and glanced at her reflection in one of the windows and sat back down. Benny noticed and smiled.

"Taking a break from your work?" Benny asked, climbing out of the car.

"Yes. I was working on some new techniques and mixed a few things together that I shouldn't have. I almost passed out in there."

"You wouldn't be the first person to pass out in there."

Nina laughed.

"I need to ask you a favor," Benny said.

"Sure."

"We had another murder." Benny watched Nina's face. It didn't change. "I was talking with Officer Kearns and we're at a point where we need to narrow our suspects. Every suspect we can eliminate helps tremendously with the legwork. I need your permission to talk to Uncle Karl's doctor."

"So, you're saying he's a suspect?" Nina seemed surprised.

"Unfortunately he is."

"Why?"

"Can I trust this information won't leave the front porch?"

"Of course. I don't have many friends outside of my family, and I rarely leave the house."

"The second murder involved art just like the first. Uncle Karl is... well, that is part of the problem. I don't completely understand *what* he is, but I do know a few things about him. He pretends to be an artist. He is wildly strange. He may do things he is not aware of, or maybe he has everybody snowed over and is willingly doing crazy things. That is my job—figuring this out. I would like to rule him out."

"So what does this favor involve?"

"It's simple. I have a piece of paper that I would like you to sign, which will give me permission to talk with his doctor. His doctor will hopefully be able to explain his condition to me a little better and I will mark him off of my list of suspects."

"Fine. I'll sign it."

Benny pulled the form out and handed it to her with a pen.

"I have another question," Nina said. "I'm an artist. Am I a suspect?"

Benny made a motion with his hand as if he was signing a document and he looked at the paper in her hand. Nina hesitated with the question still in her mind and Benny pointed to the place he needed her to sign. Nina signed and Benny pulled the paper away from her and put it away.

Finally answering her question, Benny said, "Unfortunately, yes."

Dr. Walton's office occupied the ground floor of an old two story Victorian located near Tilley's town square. He lived on the second floor with his mother. It was his childhood home. He had the same bedroom and his mother still did his laundry and cooked for him. Benny caught him just as he was about to lock the front door.

Dr. Walton pulled open the door and said, "I was just closing for the day." His eyes studied Benny. "Hey, you're the FBI guy."

"I used to be in the FBI. Now I'm helping out Officer Kearns with his investigations when he needs me."

Dr. Walton reminded Benny of an overgrown kid. He had a terrible bowl cut, inquisitive eyes, and his clothes were about two sizes too small. Benny decided he must have been at least six-feet-five at the shortest, but his silly grin made him look much smaller.

"I've seen you on television."

Benny was never completely sure how to answer this statement.

"I have been on TV a few times." As usual, Benny felt stupid with his response.

"You look bigger on television."

"They say the camera adds ten pounds," Benny tried.

"No. Not fatter. Taller."

"I'm over six feet tall."

"Hmmm..."

Benny had serious doubts that the man before him was a competent doctor.

"Do you like lamb?" Dr. Walton asked.

"They're cute. Sure. I love wool sweaters and..." Benny had no idea where this was going.

"Do you like to eat them?"

"Oh. Yes. I do like lamb chops." Benny thought it was quite an odd question.

"Mother made lamb sandwiches for dinner. Would you like to join me?"

"Sure." Benny looked at his watch and it read four o'clock. Just in case Dr. Walton misspoke, Benny asked, "Are you having a late lunch?"

"Heavens no. We have lunch at ten forty-five."

"Oh," Benny said, trying not to act too surprised.

"Follow me upstairs."

Benny immediately noticed the smell of the house. It smelled old and sterile at the same time, somehow. Nearing the top of the stairs the smell changed and although Benny had not been hungry, the aroma woke his stomach and he was now ready to eat whatever he was smelling.

"Mother," Dr. Walton called. "Set another place at the dinner table. I have a guest."

Benny followed in awe of the situation. Dr. Walton had not asked why he was visiting and didn't seem to care. Benny wondered how he always seemed to get himself into the strangest of situations.

They entered the kitchen. The table was already set for three and Benny paused. Dr. Walton's mother had her back to the two men as she was tending to something sizzling on the stove.

"Sit down, Mr. James," she said, without turning around.

He did as instructed and sat at the round wooden table. Dr. Walton's mother turned with a black skillet in hand and shoveled a hand-pressed sandwich onto Benny's plate. It looked delectable.

Benny looked up from his plate to her eyes and she gave him a wink accompanied with a warm smile. She turned back to the stove, deposited the black skillet, and picked up another. This one contained fried potatoes and she dumped a healthy portion on his plate.

"Were you expecting someone else?" Benny asked. He knew there was no way possible she could have set another place in between the time Dr. Walton called out and the time they walked into the room.

"No," Dr. Walton's mother said. "Sweet tea or water?" she asked brushing aside his curiosity.

"Ice tea, please." Benny studied her as she turned to the fridge and estimated she was late sixties or early seventies. Her skin rippled with wrinkles galore swaying Benny's guess in favor of older. Stark white hair sprung from her head and she stooped when she walked in the same manner as her son. As she placed the glass of ice tea in front of him, Benny looked into her eyes to find a youthful gleam.

"I'm Benny by the way."

"I've seen you on television."

There that statement was again and Benny had an idea of how to respond this time.

"Do I look shorter, taller, fatter, or skinnier to you in person than I do on television?"

"You look much bigger. On television, you're only about this big," she said spreading her thumb and index finger.

Benny realized she was making a joke and chuckled politely. "I didn't catch your name?"

"Hazel. Are you one of my son's patients?"

"No."

"I didn't know the two of you were friends."

"We've actually never met."

"Well then, is something wrong?" Hazel asked, suddenly alarmed.

Dr. Walton looked up from his sandwich. "I was so hungry, I didn't get around to asking Mr. James why he was here, Mother. I thought I would ask him over supper. There isn't a problem is there?"

"No. I just need to speak to you about one of your patients."

"I'm afraid that may be tricky."

"I have a consent form," Benny said, pulling the paper out.

Benny handed the paper to Dr. Walton and he set his sandwich down just long enough to study it. Nodding his head, he handed it back to Benny and filled his mouth with a load of fried potatoes.

"Karl Oglethorpe," Benny said.

Hazel dropped her fork and it struck her plate with a clang and bounced onto the table splattering the ketchup from her potatoes onto the white table cloth.

"My goodness," she said. "Excuse me."

"Was it something I said?" Benny joked.

Hazel's eyes looked frightened for a split second before she recovered and said, "Heavens no. I just bit my tongue."

"I hate it when that happens," Dr. Walton said through a mouthful. "What would you like to know about Mr. Oglethorpe?"

"Is it OK if we speak about this in front of your mother? No offense, Hazel."

"None taken. I do all the filing down there so I pretty much know everything anyway."

"Go ahead, Mr. James. I discuss my patients freely with her. She won't hear anything she probably doesn't already know."

"Very well. I'm trying to understand his condition. I want to know what you think he's capable of and I want to know how he changes when he's on or off his medications."

"Slow down, Mr. James." Dr. Walton pushed his plate away from him. Finally satiated and with a full belly he seemed like a different man. "I don't believe any of Mr. Oglethorpe's problems are medical in nature. I believe they are purely psychological."

"Then why is he not seeing a psychologist?"

"Nina believes differently and she is his legal guardian and calls the shots. So, I do what I can. Can you imagine him having a therapy session?"

"No. So, give me your theory of why he is the way he is."

"Shame. Do you know the history of the Oglethorpe place?"

"Yes, I do."

"Then you know it was once a thriving, marvelous, awe-inspiring place. It is now in shambles, barely standing and in utter disrepair. Equal rights aside for a moment, Karl is the last surviving male, not married, and with the traditional mindset, he should carry the responsibility of maintaining the family home and bringing in money. He didn't. He couldn't handle the responsibility and checked out."

"What about the mimicking? What about the fantasies of being an artist?"

"The artist fantasy lets him forgive himself for not being a good businessman. He tells himself he is the antithesis of the businessman—the free spirit artist. It's his favorite fantasy."

"I was there yesterday and he was sunburned from using an arc welder. Supposedly it wasn't the first time he did it. And, he has a studio."

"Yes, he has all the tools to be an artist—but it doesn't mean he is. I was called out to the Oglethorpe home last Thanksgiving because he had sunburned his backside severely."

"That's the story I heard."

"He had welded two pieces of metal together, but I certainly wouldn't call it art."

Hazel stood and collected the dishes from the table.

"Would either of you like some pie?"

"No, thank you," Benny answered.

"Maybe later, Mother."

Hazel put the dishes in the sink. "I'll clean these up later so you two boys can talk. I'll be in my room reading if you need me."

"I see your point," Benny said as she disappeared around the corner. "I could have all the equipment you have downstairs, but it wouldn't make me a doctor."

"Exactly. Karl's studio is just kind of a clubhouse of sorts."

"It had some good paintings in there."

"Nina puts her castaways in there. She told me when I asked the same question."

"Why does she play along? I noticed her daughter Angel does as well. Why don't they confront him?"

"Because it's an unpredictable tactic. They can live with a fake artist. What if they confront him and he decides to try on another persona?"

"OK. So, is that what he's doing when he mimics? Just trying on different personalities? Nina said after a few visits with me he would be able to mimic me perfectly."

"That's my guess. He's a unique case, that's for sure."

"What about the medications? Nina told me he can be wild when he doesn't take his meds."

"That is simply not true and something she projects onto him. Luckily, she hasn't ever researched the medications I've given him. If she did, she would discover one is for depression and the other two are basically vitamins."

"She seems to believe they're some type of antipsychotic drugs."

"They're not. Ms. Oglethorpe seems to live in a world of her own as well."

"Do you think Uncle Karl is capable of murder?"

"No. Not without leaving a trail."

"That's not very reassuring."

"I believe anybody is capable of murder, so he falls under this grand umbrella. I don't think he has the ability to cover up a murder at this point with the state of his mental health."

"Are you certain?"

"Take a close look around his studio the next time you visit. He can't even hide the fact that he didn't create the works in there. He doesn't wash his brushes. All of his pallets are filthy and filled with browns, blacks, and other dark colors. He doesn't even know how to mix paints properly. Make a point to go and look. If he can't hide that—he is definitely not your killer, Mr. James."

Benny nodded his head up and down as he thought.

"OK," he finally said. He stood. "You have been incredibly generous with your time and your home," he said sticking out his hand.

The two men shook hands.

"It was my pleasure. Come back if you think of any more questions."

Benny followed Dr. Walton back to the top of the stairs. Just as they were about to descend, the door to a room opened, and Hazel appeared.

"You sure you don't want a piece of pie, Mr. James?"

"I'm too full, but thank you," Benny said looking past her and into her bedroom.

On the wall, above her bed, was a painting covered in numbers.

Chapter 11

Benny's mouth fell and his eyes shot open wide. Hazel's did the same.

"Where did you get that painting?" he asked pointing.

"That old thing," she said accompanied by a laugh Benny processed as fake. "I don't recall."

Benny walked into the room without being invited. Sure enough, the canvas had eights painted all over its surface. He turned and walked toward Hazel. Benny stopped when he was face-to-face with her. All of his nice was gone.

"Remember, now," he instructed.

"OK. I don't want him to get into any trouble."

"Who?"

"Karl."

"And why would he get in trouble?"

"I read the paper," Hazel answered. "I know there was a painting that had numbers involved with the murder. And you think this has something to do with that. Karl would never do anything like that."

"Let the law be the judge of that," Benny said, unsuccessfully trying to find his nice again.

"I can prove it has nothing to do with numbers," Hazel said walking over to the painting.

"It's obviously full of eights," Benny huffed.

"No, it's not. I hung it the wrong way because I didn't like it the way it was meant to be." Hazel climbed on her bed at the foot and carefully made her way to the headboard. She stopped and gained her balance before pulling the painting away from the wall and rotating it to the right. She hung the painting back on the wall and climbed down from the bed.

"That's the way it's supposed to be. It's not a number. He didn't kill anybody."

Benny and Dr. Walton looked at the painting, now in its new orientation.

"I don't know if that's any better, Mother," Dr. Walton said.

"What?"

"It's the symbol for infinity," Benny said.

"So? That's not a specific number."

"I guess you're right," Benny conceded. "Sorry for my alarm. I'll show myself out."

Benny walked out shaking his head before he said something he would later regret.

Benny drove to Red's house. As usual, Red was in his garden. The giant metal sea creature flashed reflected light behind him. Red noticed the Jeep pulling into the driveway and waved, smiling broadly.

"You so hard, Bendy."

"Do you mean to say I've been working hard?"

"Yep. That what Red saying." Red pulled a bug off one of his tomato plants and squished it between his fingers.

"I don't usually correct your speech, but in this instance I have to advise you not to say that to anyone else."

"But you *is* so hard."

"Hard working," Benny tried.

"Hard working," Red repeated.

"Good. That sounds much better. I need your help."

"You need Red help to catching bad man?"

"I need some information that might help me catch him."

"OK."

"When you had the flu last year, didn't you end up going to a doctor here in town?"

"Yep. I had the monia."

"Right, pneumonia. Do you remember the doctor's name?"

"No, but Red remember he live with he mama."

"Dr. Walton?"

"Yep. That be hims. But he not a bad man."

"I'm not saying he's a bad man. I just wanted to know what you thought of him?"

"I not like he mama."

"Why?"

"She say mean things 'cause Red not having assurance. And she not taking cornbread."

"I know you don't have insurance, but you tried to pay her with cornbread?"

"It very good. It be Mama secret cornbread."

"Red," Benny said trying not to smile, "doctors don't usually barter and you have *lots* of money in the bank."

"The man at the farmcy trade little medicines for peach pie."

"Oh my God, Red! You have five hundred thousand dollars in the bank."

"You tell Red to spend careful."

"I meant, don't go out and buy a helicopter."

"Red not knowing how to ride a helicopter."

"Never mind. Uncle Karl gave Dr. Walton's mother a painting. Do you know why?"

"Nope. Maybe they taking paintings but not cornbread."

"Maybe. Have you ever been in Uncle Karl's studio when he's painting?"

"I think he the world slowest painter." Red pulled another bug off a plant and squeezed it between his fingers. It made a popping noise."

"Why don't you buy some bug spray?"

"Vegables not liking that."

"So, you have seen Uncle Karl paint?"

"No, he just mix he paints together to make ugly colors."

"Maybe he's lying and he can't paint," Benny suggested.

"That crazy, Bendy."

"The world's full of crazy people, Red."

"I think Bendy know most of them."

"I think I do."

The next morning Benny drove over to the police station to see if it was back to normal and it was. Vernon was at his desk poring over documents and Chief Neighbors was in his office with the door closed. Strange animal-like noises seeped under the door and out into the area beyond.

"What's going on back there?" Benny asked.

"The usual. A short-haired brunette stress reliever. The hair color and length change, but the rest seems to stay the same."

A loud grunt filled the room accompanied by the sounds of someone being chased and squealing.

"I've got a surprise for you," Vernon said.

"What?"

Vernon pointed to a closed laptop sitting on his desk.

"You bought me a computer? You know I don't like those things."

"I didn't buy you a computer. It came out of our first vic's car."

"And why is it on your desk and not in evidence? You know it takes the state forever to get to small towns like this. We need to get this thing processed and in line."

"I thought we could give Ned a crack at it first—without telling anyone he did, of course."

Benny's eyes lit up and he nodded with a smile streaking across his face.

Ned was Benny's go-to guy for all things computer related. He was one part techno-genius and two parts mad scientist. Ned could infiltrate any government website and could somehow find more information than any state or federal database. Ned was by far one of the strangest people he had ever met.

"I've been meaning to get over to Ned's," Benny said. "I've been afraid to go over there ever since he told me about the mushroom farm he's constructed in his basement. I know I'm going to have to take a tour of it and I can't even begin to tell you how much I detest mushrooms. Even the sight of them makes me sick, and for some reason he can't get it in his thick skull that I hate them. He is always trying to make me mushroom pizza or give me bags of mushrooms he made in his closet—I'm starting to feel sick just talking about them."

"They're really good," Vernon tried.

"Mushrooms?"

"Ned's mushrooms. He sells them to the grocery store over by my house."

Benny picked up the laptop off Vernon's desk and said, "I'm not so sure we're friends anymore."

Ned's driveway stretched at least a half-mile. Benny had never made a surprise visit to Ned's and wondered what unusual activity he might find upon his arrival. Usually when Benny called that he was coming, Ned taped a note to the door with instructions on where to find him. On this day the door was wide open.

Benny thought the open door was unusual and quietly closed the door to the Jeep. He crept toward the front door and listened. As he inched forward he heard Ned screaming in pain. Benny took off running.

Entering the house, Benny found the place to be unusually messy. From Benny's past experience he knew that Ned had a messy mind but kept a pretty neat house. As Benny passed the foyer he heard another scream toward the back of the house. He ran in the direction of the noise.

When Benny entered the solarium at the back of the house he found Ned on the floor shocking himself with what was obviously a homemade device.

"What in God's name are you doing?" Benny screamed.

Ned looked up with surprise and put down the device. His head dropped and bounced on the hardwood floor.

"Just a study," Ned said, drooling.

"A study on what? What a dumbass you are?"

"No. A study on pain and its effects on the brain."

"I hope I'm dreaming," Benny said, as he stood over Ned.

Ned looked as though he hadn't showered in days. His hair looked like it hadn't been brushed in months and his skin was pale. His lips trembled.

"So let me get this straight. You are shocking yourself with some crazy thing you made to study pain?"

"Basically."

Benny shook his head. "Why don't you stand up and I'll kick your ass for being so stupid and then you can study how that feels?"

"Would you really do that for me?" Ned asked, trying to smile but drooling some more.

"No!"

"Please, Benny. Just punch me once."

Not able to control his anger at the situation, Benny kicked Ned in the stomach. Ned made a noise like he was going to throw up and breathed out hard.

"Thank you so much," he said. Ned climbed up off the ground. As he stood, his body shook and convulsed.

"Are you OK?"

"Never been better. Thank you."

"I'm sorry I kicked you. I've had a long day and it just happened."

"I'm glad you did and I thank and forgive you at the same time."

"I think I appreciate that."

"Did you come for mushrooms?"

"No."

"You haven't seen the farm!" Ned said, suddenly remembering that Benny had not been given a tour.

Still feeling bad about kicking him in the stomach, Benny replied, "No, I haven't. Will you please give me a tour?" He could not believe the words that had just escaped his lips.

"Gladly," Ned said, stumbling toward the basement door.

The mushroom farm was just as disgusting as Benny had imagined. There were mushrooms growing on rotten logs, piles of manure, and other substances that looked to Benny like disease and filth.

"How about a taste test?"

"No! Um... I'm fasting."

"OK. I'll have to give you a rain check."

"I hope I don't lose it," Benny said, heading for the steps to go back upstairs.

Back upstairs, he changed the subject and asked Ned if he would take a look at the laptop for him.

"As usual, anything we find out together is a secret."

"If I tell anyone will you come back over and beat me up?"

"Nice try. Very funny."

Ned took the laptop to his desk and opened it.

"It's password protected," Ned said, mumbling. His fingers flew across the keys and it looked to Benny as if he were giving the keyboard a secret handshake with all the different key combinations he was pushing so quickly. "That was easy," he mumbled again.

"Um," Benny said. "Excuse me, Ned." Ned looked up. "Don't you need to know what to look for?"

Ned laughed. "The computer will tell me and I'll let you know."

"Huh?"

Ned punched more keys and Benny made himself comfortable in the chair across from his desk.

Ned looked up a few minutes later and said, "I think I have a pretty clear picture of what's going on here. The owner of this computer is named Alton."

"Was."

Ned shot Benny a look and nodded. "Let me begin again. The owner of this computer *was* named Alton. Last name, Barnes. He recently mapquested directions from an address in Brunswick, Georgia to

Tilley. I see a few other hits here from Brunswick, so I'm guessing he resided there." Ned typed a few more keys and said, "Yep, I found his home address and it's the same. Real smart guy, he was keeping a copy of last year's tax returns on his desktop in a folder called tax returns." Ned laughed like he had told a hilarious joke. "What a moron." Blood started running out of Ned's nose and Benny jumped up.

"Ned, get away from the computer. I can wipe your fingerprints off it before I turn it over to the state, but getting your blood off it might be a different story."

"I feel woozy," Ned said. "And really, real, thirty. I'm thirty!" he screamed. Ned tried to stand and stumbled backward. "I'm thirty!" he yelled again. "Thirsty," he was finally able to say before he toppled over and passed out.

Chapter 12

Benny dragged Ned to a couch. He was still out cold. Benny ran to the fridge and yanked the door open looking for a bottle of water. Unimaginable concoctions and mushrooms stared back at him along with a few other things he thought he saw move. Toward the back of the fridge, a lone bottle of water hid behind a wet glove. Benny carefully reached for the bottle trying not to think why a wet glove might be in Ned's fridge. He carefully examined the bottle in case Ned was storing God-knows-what in the bottle instead of water and decided the seal had not been broken. He opened it and sniffed. No smell. Benny decided it must be water.

Running back to the couch, Benny almost tripped over the homemade device Ned had built to shock himself. He checked on Ned who was still out, sat the bottle of water next to him, and went back for the shocking device. Benny picked it up and carried it into the kitchen.

In the kitchen, he pulled open drawers until he found a pair of scissors. The same drawer also contained a pair of pliers. Benny put the device on the kitchen table and studied it. It had twenty or so wires sticking up and out from all directions with differing colors.

Unsure whether he would shock himself or not, Benny held his breath as he chose a red wire and cut. Nothing happened. He cut a blue one. Nothing. A yellow. Smoke. With one eye closed, he began snipping furiously at wire after wire as the device hummed and whistled and spewed. Finally, with the room filled with smoke, it stopped. Benny heard coughing.

He ran to Ned as he sat bolt upright. "Thirty!" he screamed.

"Thirsty," Benny corrected, handing him the bottle of water. Ned grabbed it and poured it down his throat. Benny watched, amazed that almost all the water went in his mouth.

Ned let out a tremendous sigh.

"You were really thirty."

"You killed it," Ned said. "I smell the smoke."

"Yes, I killed it. If you rebuild it, I will kill *you*. I will destroy the mushroom farm, and I will... oh God Ned, just please stop being so weird."

"OK. It was a good study," Ned tried.

"No, it wasn't. It was almost as stupid as someone having a wet glove in their refrigerator."

"That's the glove I touched Steven Hawking with."

"And why is it wet?"

"Secret."

"Fine. I have a feeling I don't want to know."

"You don't."

"Can we change the subject?"

"Do you want to know what else I found in the computer?"

"Please."

"I found a screenshot for a Craigslist ad."

"What's Craigslist?"

"Are you kidding me?"

Benny shook his head from side to side.

"It's like classifieds on the computer. And before you ask, a screenshot is like taking a picture of what is on your computer screen."

"So, Alton basically had a picture of a classified ad?"

"Yes."

"And what did it say?"

"The writer of the ad wanted someone for a 'curious adventure.' It said something that sounded sexual and maybe about drugs—you have to read it. It's strange. You can read it one way as completely innocent and another way as something different."

"When you're able to stand up and function again, can you pull it back up on the computer and show it to me?"

"I'm one step ahead of you. I already sent it to the printer. You know where my printer is, right?"

"Yes," Benny answered rolling his eyes so Ned couldn't see. "It's under the framed gun that was used to shoot Ronald Regan."

"Right."

Ned claimed and really did believe he owned the gun that was used in the Regan shooting. Benny had never told Ned he didn't believe him and didn't want to have that conversation or hear about how he acquired it again, so he hurried off to the other room.

Benny pulled the paper off the printer and read:

Seeking male for curious adventure. Must be willing to think outside the box and play in the box.

Will be rewarded with candy and sugar. Must be a big dog who loves cats.

"What?" Benny said aloud.

"Benny?" Ned called from the other room.

Benny scampered back into the room.

"I don't mean to be rude, but can we finish this all later? I think a nap would do me some good."

"Sure. How about I stick around just in case you need some sort of help?"

"I don't think that's necessary. One of the reasons I'm off is probably because I've been awake for fifty-nine hours."

"Fifty-nine hours!"

"Just another part of the study."

"Somebody should study you. I'll leave, but you have to promise to call me if you wake up not feeling well."

"OK."

"Can I just leave the computer here and we can wrap this up tomorrow?"

"Yes," Ned said, nodding off and snapping his head back up.

"See you tomorrow." Before Benny even finished his sentence Ned was asleep.

Back at the Tilley Police Station, Vernon was still working at his desk.

"Any luck?"

"Maybe. Ned's a little tired and is taking a nap, so hopefully it will be all right if I get the computer back to you tomorrow."

"Sure. I think if we get it processed before the end of business tomorrow nobody will ever be the wiser. Hell, he can keep it two more days if he needs to. We'll just put in the report that we discovered it tomorrow."

"Gotta love small towns, huh?"

"They're the best." Benny unfolded the piece of paper from Ned's printer. "I need your help with some lingo on a document we found on Alton's computer."

"I'll try."

"Let me read you the Craigslist ad we found. 'Seeking male for curious adventure. Must be willing to think outside the box and play in the box. Will be rewarded with candy and sugar. Must be a big dog who loves cats.'"

Vernon laughed. "Let's call in the expert on this one." He turned his head toward Chief Neighbors' office and yelled, "Chief. Need your help out here."

Chief Neighbors emerged from behind his office door rubbing his eyes.

"You sleeping in there?"

"Yeah. I got a big date tonight."

"But this week you've already been with two... never mind. Give him the paper and let him read it," he instructed Benny.

Benny handed Chief Neighbors the copy of the ad and both men watched him read. The Chief's eyes widened and began to glow.

"Did it come with a phone number? E-mail address?"

"It's a piece of evidence in the murder case," Benny said, snatching the paper out of his hands.

The glow from Chief Neighbors' eyes vanished.

"Of course," he said, obviously dejected.

"What does all that mean?" Benny asked. "I understand thinking outside the box, but what does 'play in the box' mean?"

"A box is a woman's entertainment center," Chief Neighbors said. "How does anybody not know that?"

Benny shrugged his shoulders.

"What about the candy and sugar part?" Vernon asked.

"Well, sugar is nookie. I've heard people call cocaine 'nose candy.' They were probably talking about that."

"We were thinking in the same vein," Vernon said. "What about the big dog and cats part?"

"A cat would most probably be a woman and a dog would be a man. So maybe she likes big men."

"Thanks, Chief," Vernon said, excusing him. Chief Neighbors took the cue and disappeared back behind his office door.

"He scares me," Benny said. "Is he part rabbit?"

"Must be." Vernon's face turned serious. "So, we have a hunter. Not only does our killer enjoy the kill, he also enjoys the set-up."

"You think we're looking for a male?"

"Yeah, don't you? I think it's a guy pretending to be a girl."

"I'm still open to either one, but I'm leaning toward your way of thinking."

"Well, this piece of information might convolute your thinking." Vernon handed Benny a sheet of paper from his desk.

As Benny studied the paper, his eyes doubled in size.

"Victim number two," Vernon said. "The guy in the ice cooler."

"I'll be damned. Erick Frederickson, also known as Little E. Big E's brother."

"Yes, it is."

"I thought he was incarcerated in Colorado."

"Seems as though he was paroled last week."

"Do you think Big E knows?"

"Knows what? That his brother is dead or that he was paroled?"

"Either one," Benny said handing the paper back to Vernon.

"I have a feeling he knows both."

"Let's go find out."

"Chief isn't going to like us bothering him again."

"Well, tough. At least we now have a real reason."

Benny drove and Vernon thought out loud as they made their way to the other side of the lake and Big E's monstrous office.

"Let's just say that Big E knew his brother was getting out of jail. Or, maybe he didn't know and was surprised to find him on his doorstep asking for his half of the family money."

"Wouldn't he have called?"

"Benny," Vernon admonished, "I'm trying to think something through here."

"Sorry, I'll just shut up and drive."

"Thanks." Vernon stared out the window and continued. "Either way, Big E probably wanted him out of the picture. So, maybe Big E told Little E he would cut him his half of the money if he killed Alton, all the while knowing he would double-cross him."

"But," Benny tried.

"Shh! I'm not finished. And he needed Rene's help, so he..."

"Can we just ask him some questions and go from there?"

"Dammit Benny. I almost had it figured out."

"Sure you did. And what about the art? How does that play into it all?"

"I was getting there."

"No you weren't."

"I was. They threw in the art stuff to put suspicion on Nina Oglethorpe and Uncle Karl since they are the town weirdoes."

"Touché," Benny said. "Next time you have some out loud thinking to do, why don't we take separate vehicles?" Benny cackled and playfully punched Vernon in the arm.

Pulling into Big E's driveway the two men witnessed a golf cart ascending the hill from the dock area below.

"Poor golf cart," Vernon commented.

Big E noticed the Jeep and his jowls sunk.

"I don't think he's happy to see us," Benny said. "Do you want to play good cop, bad cop?"

"Nah. Let's play bad cop, bad cop."

"That's fun too. You lead and I'll follow."

Vernon got out of the car first and slammed the door extra hard to make a statement. He looked pissed and Benny tried not to show his amusement.

Big E parked the golf cart and wiggled out. "I thought we settled our business about the gambling. I'll have you know I am a very good friend of Chief Neighbors and he is going to hear about this visit."

"He's the one who sent us," Vernon lied, filling his chest with a deep breath.

"Oh?"

"Yeah. We're on to more serious things today. That gambling is petty bullshit compared to what we're onto today."

Benny stepped in front of Vernon and said, "I thought the Chief said to cuff this asshole and drag him into the station."

"He did," Vernon lied, playing along. "I just want to hear what he has to say for himself here and now. I'm an impatient man and I'm ready to get at the truth *now*."

"The truth about what?" Big E asked.

"Oh, hell no. He didn't just say that, did he?" Vernon asked.

"He did."

"I really don't know," Big E pleaded.

"We aren't stupid, boy. Yeah, I called you boy. Ironic ain't it? You go to the Chief and complain about me being up in your grill and you call *me* boy. Chief Neighbors may be a lot of things, but he is loyal and he told me about that. Boy? What is this? 1950?"

"I'm sorry. I was angry about the gambling thing."

"Why don't you drop all the hateful bullshit and tell me a little something about your brother."

"Erick?"

"No, your other brother, dummy. You only have one brother. Spill."

"He's in prison."

Benny pushed Vernon aside and said, "We all know that isn't true. This may be a small town, but we still have access to phone records. You better think about this next answer long and hard before you give it because I'm going to hold you to it in court."

"Court?"

"You heard me," Benny said, gritting his teeth together in Big E's face. "When is the last time your brother called you? And remember, I probably already know the answer."

"Jesus. OK. I talked to him last week. He said he was probably getting paroled."

"And?"

"That's it. He said he would come home and wondered if I could give him any work. I told him I could."

"You weren't angry?" Vernon asked.

"Why would I be angry?"

"Money."

"He has a trust account that is worth at least three million dollars," Big E stated.

"Then why would he be inquiring about work?" Benny asked.

"It was a requirement of his parole. He had to find a steady job to keep him busy I guess."

"And have you heard from him since?"

"No. He does this all the time. He makes contact and he drops off the face of the earth."

"What if I told you he was dead," Vernon said.

"I would tell you I wasn't surprised."

"It's true," Benny said. "We found your brother dead yesterday."

"He was a scoundrel," Bid E said. "I won't miss him."

"What did you have to do with it?" Vernon said trying to get his edge back, but feeling sorrow for Big E's loss.

"Nothing. Nothing at all."

Big E's face was a blank. Neither Benny nor Vernon could read anything at all in the expression that it held.

"I'm sorry for your loss," Benny said. "His body is at the county morgue and Chief Neighbors was supposed to contact your parents this afternoon."

"They won't be surprised," Big E said solemnly.

Vernon tipped his head toward the car as he caught Benny's eye, signaling he was ready to leave. Benny shook his head side to side signaling no. With Big E looking away, Benny pointed to his head signaling back to Vernon that he had an idea.

"If I can use your restroom real fast, we'll be out of your hair and on our way."

"Sure," Big E said, waving Benny toward the house. Vernon waited in the driveway.

Benny pretended to rush toward the bathroom. He flushed the toilet after a minute and turned on the sink faucets. Finished pretending, he emerged from the restroom and took a look around the decorated room and out the window onto the lake below..

"My God," he said to Big E. "What a view. And look at this art."

"I am blessed," Bid E said.

A painting caught Benny's eye and he walked toward it.

"Ah," Big E said as Benny stood in front of it. "My favorite."

Benny studied it and his eyes finally made their way to the painted signature—Nina Oglethorpe.

Chapter 13

"Why did you want to go inside of Big E's place so bad?" Vernon asked on the drive back to the station.

"I thought I might be able to tell with a quick look around if Little E had been there or not."

"Big E said he hadn't seen or heard from him since the phone call."

"And I'm pretty sure he's lying. The door frame is splintered and a piece of drywall just inside the door is cracked as if someone forced their way in and had a bit of a tussle just inside the door. The rest of the place is immaculate. Big E doesn't seem like the kind of person to let something like that go unrepaired. I bet if we go back in a few days it will be repaired and good as new."

"Do you think Little E really has a three million dollar trust fund?"

"I'm guessing no. Why don't you dig around on that one. And did you ever run the registration number on the boat?"

"No, I'll do both of those things this afternoon. I guess I better tell Chief Neighbors what we're up to as well before he gets another phone call and loses his mind."

"Maybe without Big E's donation money you could beat him in the next election."

"Stop saying that," Vernon warned. "I've actually started thinking about the possibility."

"You got my vote." Benny bobbed his head and bit his lip as he tried to hide his grin. He knew he was responsible for putting the thought into Vernon's mind.

Benny dropped Vernon off at the station and headed back toward the Oglethorpe place as he had thought of a few questions he wanted to ask Uncle Karl. He also just wanted the opportunity to observe him with his new understanding of his ability to mimic others. Benny also hoped to have the opportunity to explain to Nina that he wasn't the fainting type.

Uncle Karl was throwing rocks at a dead pine tree when he arrived. Getting out of the Jeep he noticed a kite was stuck between some branches.

"The m... m... man is kee... keeping me down," Uncle Karl stuttered.

"The way I see it, a tree is keeping you down."

Although Nina and Dr. Walton had told him of Uncle Karl's ability to switch personalities and mimic other people, Benny had not truly believed. He watched Uncle Karl in amazement as even the way he moved was different. Benny wondered who he was mimicking.

"Pick up a ro... ro... rock and help. Stop standing around and wa... wa... wasting my time." Uncle Karl glared at Benny and even his eyes seemed to be different. The man whom Benny had talked to before was not behind the eyes he looked into.

Benny picked up a handful of rocks and began to throw. He hit the kite a few times, but it didn't budge. Picking up a stick, Benny hurled it toward the kite and realized midair it probably wasn't the best idea he'd ever had. The stick pierced the cheap kite, going all the way through it while the kite remained stuck in the tree.

"You little bi... bi... bitch," Uncle Karl screamed. "Get out of my fa... fa... fa... face! N... n... now!"

Benny hurried back to the Jeep and sped off as Uncle Karl pounded his chest like a mad gorilla.

As Benny made his way back into town he passed the Lakeside Motor Inn and noticed the parking lot was beginning to accumulate vans from various media outlets across the country. During the last murder case, which rocked the little town, the lot was full and every room was filled with some sort of journalist. Benny slowed the Jeep and spied Room 12—the room Rachael had stayed in when he met her. His heart lurched and without thinking he pulled the vehicle into the lot and parked in front of the door. As he stared at the door he wondered what she was doing and if she was thinking of him. Thoughts of her vanished as someone tapped on the driver's side window. Benny broke from his thoughts. He lowered the window.

"We don't allow loitering."

"How do you do, Carlton?"

Carlton was the owner of the hotel and ran it with the help of his family. He was a retired businessman who had traveled extensively during his career. Once retired, he decided to build an Inn that had all the things he wanted in a room but never got all those years on the road.

"She was a good one," Carlton offered.

"You heard, huh?"

"You know Donny can't keep his mouth shut. He's pretty upset. How're you doing?"

"I'm OK. I obviously miss her—I'm sitting in my car in front of a room she stayed in a couple of years ago. How sad is that?"

"Heartache makes a person do strange things. Do you want me to go get the key for you so you can go inside?"

"No, but that's really kind of you to offer, Carlton. I'd rather just sit here and imagine her inside."

"Do whatever it takes and stay as long as you like. If you change your mind about the key, you know where to find me."

"Thanks."

"Oh," Carlton said, "have you been by Rene's today?"

"No, why?"

"A newspaper guy from Ohio was in the lobby earlier saying a New York City art dealer was there causing a stir. He was buying all the paintings off the wall. Cleaned out the entire restaurant."

"What?"

"I guess he's thinking he can get a piece of history if he buys a piece of art made by a killer. If the killer you're looking for is a local artist or using their work, their other work might fetch a pretty penny."

"That's sick."

"People will pay big bucks for crazy things."

"I better get over there."

Carlton waved as Benny put the Jeep in reverse and backed away from Room 12.

The parking lot at Rene's was nearly full. Gawkers and media types filled the restaurant and just as Carlton had described, the once filled walls were bare. Benny found one of the few empty seats and sat down.

He ordered a beer and asked the waitress to tell Rene he would like to speak to her. Rene delivered his beer and sat down with a smile on her face.

"On the house," she said.

"What are you so happy about?"

"Don't you see?" she said waving her arms, "I sold it all."

"Didn't you tell me you do this out of the goodness of your heart and you don't make any commission?"

"That *was* true. I have now instituted a new policy and procedure that requires a 50/50 split for displaying and selling your paintings and other art pieces here."

"That's convenient," Benny said, taking a swig from his beer.

Rene huffed. "I know what this looks like to you, but I have bills to pay and you know me better than to think I would have anything at all to do with anything evil."

"You're right and I apologize for insinuating that anything nefarious is going on here. For years you've provided a great service to the local artists and you have the right to profit from this opportunity."

"Thank you. And we're jacking up the prices big time on the next batch," she said, with a mischievous wink and smile.

"Where are you going to get more?"

"Benny, these artists have stacks of canvases at their homes and studios. I've already called all of them and requested more."

"And they're all on board for the 50/50 split?"

"Yes. They were all tickled pink that their work sold today, and I told them we would double the prices so it wouldn't be like they were losing any money at all with the new agreement."

"Brilliant."

"I gotta run," Rene said. "Channel 11 wants to interview me for the evening news and I need to rehearse what I'm going to say and check my face."

"Thanks for the beer," Benny said, holding up the bottle.

Benny pulled his cell phone out of his pocket and called Vernon.

"Yo," Vernon answered.

"You busy?"

"No, now that Chief Neighbors is finished yelling at me I don't know what to do with myself."

"Was it that bad when you told him we questioned Big E?"

"Worse than you could even imagine. Try to imagine an angry person having a nervous breakdown, a psychotic episode, and a seizure all at the same time and you might start to get a mental picture of what it was like."

"Ouch. Can I buy you a beer? I'm at Rene's."

"On my way."

Benny ordered two more and before he knew it, Vernon sat down with questions written all over his face. Benny got him up to speed.

"So, who does the new development throw the most suspicion on?" Vernon asked.

"Rene, Nina, Uncle Karl, and everybody else who's going to profit from this new gold rush on the Tilley art scene." Benny drank from his new beer. "Oh, listen to what happened to me earlier. I went to see Uncle Karl this afternoon and he was a different person."

"He was what?"

"Remember how I told you he has the ability to mimic other personalities?"

"Yeah."

"Well, I went by there today and he was angry and stuttering."

"I don't know anybody who stutters. I do know a lot of angry people."

Benny laughed and almost spit out a mouthful of beer.

Changing the subject, Vernon said, "I did run the registration number on the boat Big E was in and the number doesn't come up in the system. It's weird. The number doesn't even exist."

"I just don't see how he fits into this."

"Maybe he doesn't."

"It's just too coincidental that Little E is involved," Benny said.

A drunk girl stumbled by their table and stopped. "Did you just say Little E?"

"Yes," Benny and Vernon answered at the same time.

She wobbled and said, "Thank God they locked up that stuttering asshole."

Chapter 14

The following morning Benny woke up unusually early again and began to worry. *I never wake up early and this is two days in a row. What is wrong with me?* His first thoughts turned to Ned and he wondered how his night had been and if he was fully recovered.

Benny's usual routine was to get a cup of coffee and the paper from Donny in the marina's office, but after his last performance, Benny was unsure whether he wanted the drama. Benny checked his personal coffee reserves and found they were empty. He headed out the door and up the dock toward the office and Donny.

Opening the door, Benny took a deep breath and entered the marina office.

"I feel better today," Donny said.

"I'm glad," Benny answered, walking toward the coffee pot.

"It was just such a shock."

"It was for me too. Do you want to talk about it?" Benny hoped he didn't.

"No," Donny said, sucking back tears. "Too soon."

"I understand," Benny said, with a consoling voice. "Let me know when you're ready."

"OK." Tears welled up behind his eyes.

Benny grabbed the paper and headed back to his boat shaking his head.

Back on the top deck, Benny eased into a rocker. The sun peeked above the horizon. Benny read in the paper about the new art rush in Tilley.

He thought it was written as if the murders had taken a back seat to the art. Benny's heart began to beat wildly and he noticed he was gritting his teeth. He wanted to be angry, but wasn't sure who to be angry with. Whenever Benny felt this way, the only person who could bring perspective back into his life was Red. Benny rarely called him, but decided he needed to hear a voice of reason and dialed Red's number.

"Red here."

"Red?" Benny asked, as he could barely hear anything.

"Red here," Red repeated.

"You have the phone upside down Red," Benny yelled.

Red flipped the phone around and asked, "How that, Bendy?"

"Great. I thought we drew pictures on the phone so you would know which side is for your ear and which side is for your mouth?"

"Red get a new phone."

"Oh."

"You not can wash a phone in the wash machine."

"You tried to wash your phone in the washing machine?"

"Yep. When Red had the monia, the doctor say to Red he need to wash he phone and toothbrush. Red toothbrush be OK when he get out of wash machine, but phone not keep working. Red doctor confuse."

"He meant to wash the phone with alcohol."

"Why he not say that?"

"I don't know."

"Why Bendy awake early than squirrel? You must be worry."

"You know me well."

"No worry, Bendy. Red help you catching bad man."

"I know you'll help me any way you can, buddy."

"Red already help."

"You did?"

"Red do. You tell Red to interagaze Uncle Karl and Red do."

"You interrogated him?"

"Yep. Uncle Karl having new friend who talk more funny than Red."

"You don't talk funny, Red."

"Red know he not the same as Bendy."

"I still think you're perfect."

"I know Bendy do. But Uncle Karl friend have trouble saying he words. And he not nice."

"What do you mean?" Benny took a sip of coffee.

"He yell at Uncle Karl and ask he for money."

"What do you mean by he talks funny?"

"He get stuck on he words."

"How so?"

"If he go to say you name—he say B... B... Bendy."

"He stutters!"

"If that mean he get stuck on he words, yep."

"If I showed you a picture of him would you be able to identify him?"

"Red know him if he see he again."

"I'm going to swing by the police station and pick up his picture and I'll be over in a few minutes."

Benny dropped the phone, abandoned his cup of coffee, and hit the dock running.

Red was waiting on the front porch with a steaming cup of coffee in his hand. Benny handed him the picture and Red traded for the cup of coffee.

Red glanced at the picture. "Yep, that be he."

"I was afraid so. He's dead. One of the murder victims."

"Red not be happy that any people be dead, but Red not sad."

"When was the first time you met him?"

"Maybe six day ago. Red ride he bike to Uncle Karl house for borrow yellow paint. Art store be having they light out."

"So, last Sunday."

"That what Red say. Six day ago."

"You sure did. Was he already there when you got there or did he show up later?"

"He there. Red hear he yell at Uncle Karl from outside. He say he need monies."

"Were you scared?"

"No. Red angry. When Red angry he scare go away. Red tell funny talky man go away."

"Did he?"

"Yep. He call Red atarded and he leave."

"Did Uncle Karl talk about him any more after he left?"

"Nope. He just saying he not having much monies."

"Does he know you have a lot of money?"

"Red not thinking so."

"I know we've talked about this before, but there are a lot of bad people in the world, Red. Some might even pretend to be your friend and seem nice."

Red cut him off before he could continue. "Red know. Red know. Red not tell anybody about he $500,000 Bendy get for he."

"OK, buddy. I didn't think you would."

"Red not forget. I not atarded." Red flashed a smile.

"Thanks for the coffee. Can I bring the cup back to you later?"

"Yep. Red know Bendy need he coffee."

Benny headed back to his car feeling both better and worse about the day ahead all at the same time.

As Benny drove down the Oglethorpe's long dirt driveway he met the ice cream truck as it was leaving. He decided Uncle Karl must be having his dairy based breakfast. Instead of pulling to the side so the truck could pass, Benny steered the Jeep to the middle of the narrow lane and put the vehicle in park. The ice cream truck slowed and Benny waved as he walked to the driver side window. The driver let the window down.

"I'm not really open yet," the driver said, "but if you really want something I guess I can oblige."

"If you're not really open, then what are you doing driving way out of your way to sell two ice cream cones to a crazy old man?"

"Boss's orders."

"And who may I ask is that?"

"Mr. Frederickson."

"Big E?"

"Yeah. I don't call him that though, I call him Mr. Frederickson."

"How long have you worked for him?"

"This is my first summer. Am I in some sort of trouble?" The young driver who looked barely old enough to own a license furrowed his brow with worry.

"No," Benny said, trying to summon up a fake laugh. "Consider me a nosey neighbor."

"OK. Because I need this job. I bought a Camero on payments and if I miss even one day of work selling these cones and stuff, I might miss my payment. My dad co-signed and he told me if I miss one he's gonna take it out on me with his belt."

"Sounds like a nice guy."

"Oh, he isn't that bad. He just wasn't too sure about letting me get a new car seeing as I've never held down a job for more than a few months at a time."

"Does he understand that people aren't going to be buying ice cream in January?"

"I didn't think of that and don't think he did either."

"Something to think about."

"Yeah," the kid said, scratching his head looking puzzled.

"Let me ask you a personal question," Benny said as he reached in through the ice cream truck's driver side window and turned the ignition key off. The kid didn't flinch.

"OK."

"How much is your monthly payment?"

Without missing a beat the kid answered, "$376.52"

"I'm guessing the car isn't *brand* new?"

"No. Only has 52,000 miles on it."

"Sounds like you got a great deal," Benny lied. "How would you like to put one of those payments in your back pocket?"

"I'm not sure I know what you mean."

"Let's just say the ice cream business doesn't work out for you and you find yourself looking for work. Unable to work you will be unable to collect a paycheck. With no paycheck, you're going to miss your payment and get that dreaded belt your loving father was talking about."

"Yeah."

"What if you had an envelope with $376.52 in it in case that ever happened. You wouldn't miss your payment and you would avoid the belt."

"Well, how would I get an envelope with that much money in it?"

Benny smiled. He tried to over-exaggerate the smile, but the kid didn't pick up on the hint.

"Did I say something funny?" the kid asked.

"No." Benny thought he was perfect for the job he had in mind as he was too stupid to connect any dots, no matter how easy they might be to connect. On a sad note, Benny knew the kid would never own the Camero outright and hoped he enjoyed it for the short time the bank would allow him to drive it around.

Chapter 15

When Benny finally made it to Uncle Karl's, Karl had already devoured his two ice cream breakfast. Benny wondered who he would be today.

Benny knocked on the open studio door and entered to find Uncle Karl rubbing his chin in thought.

"Let me ask you a question," Uncle Karl said turning to Benny.

"OK."

Uncle Karl walked toward Benny with a particularly familiar trot. He slowed as he neared him. His gaze tightened and his mouth tensed. His eyes focused and he stood still.

"Why don't you tell me what you know about the situation." Uncle Karl's stare did not waver.

"I don't know what you're talking about," Benny tried.

Uncle Karl kept his gaze on Benny and pulled his hand to his hip as if he were reaching for a gun. "I don't like losing my cool, but you're about out of chances to stay on my good side." Uncle Karl cocked his head and Benny felt a wave of déjà vu.

"What?"

"Listen. We can either do this the hard way or my way."

It clicked. Uncle Karl was Benny. Benny wondered what would happen if he gave it right back to him.

Benny put his hand on his own hip and inched his fingers up toward the holster position. "I don't think we're understanding each other, and I'm afraid things are about to turn ugly here," Benny said.

"I live for ugly."

"Me too."

The two men lunged toward each other. Benny was surprised by Uncle Karl's strength as he threw him backward into one of the posts supporting the bell atop the roof. Benny grabbed at the air as he fell, only to clutch the hanging rope. As he bounced on the ground the rope tightened around his fist and the bell rang loudly, disturbing the quiet morning.

Benny popped up as Uncle Karl hovered above him. Benny hit him like a lineman making a block and Uncle Karl tumbled backward into a stack of canvases. Not wanting to hurt the old man, Benny paused as Uncle Karl's eyes adjusted and flashed. Uncle Karl grabbed a long wooden paintbrush on the ground next to him with two hands and snapped it over his knee producing a skewer with a ragged tip. Not waiting for him to act, Benny dove on top of him and pinned his arms to the ground. With wild eyes, Uncle Karl inhaled and flexed as if he were about to spit in Benny's face. Benny, still holding Uncle Karl's hands on the ground, pulled his head back and head butted him directly in the nose.

Uncle Karl screamed in pain as Angel came bolting through the door of the studio.

"I heard the bell, what's the ..."

Benny took two steps back and held his hands up. "It's not what it looks like."

Uncle Karl continued screaming as blood gushed from his nose. "Bendy is a bad, bad man." Uncle Karl changed personalities again.

"I can explain," Benny said to Angel.

"I'm sure you can, Mr. James. Before you do though, can you run into the house and get my mother and a wet wash cloth?"

"Certainly," Benny said, sprinting toward the house.

Opening the front door, Benny tried not to sound too urgent as he yelled, "Nina!" Nothing. Benny took a few more steps into the old house and tried again. "Nina!" Again, nothing. Feeling the urgency of the moment, Benny hurried back to where he remembered her studio was and threw the door open. Nina barely noticed the intrusion as she was deep in thought, hovering over a painting on the floor below her.

"Nina," Benny tried again.

She turned to him and he could see in her eyes and face that she hadn't slept in days. She probably wouldn't have heard a jet plane if it crashed into the other end of her studio. She was zonked and in some sort of zone.

"We need you outside."

She looked like she was still dreaming. Benny looked to the floor before running back outside. She had been dropping sand onto a canvas filled with numbers. The numbers were the metal kind one could buy for their mailbox and screw to the side. They had obviously been glued on and painted over numerous times. Nina dropped her bag of sand and followed Benny.

Back outside, Uncle Karl was up and didn't remember anything of the confrontation he had earlier with Benny. Blood still flowed from his nose. Benny walked toward him and put a wet washcloth from the house to his nose. He didn't seem to remember having the previous battle with Benny and let him take him into his care.

"For taking care to me I give you one thousand tomatoes."

Nina seemed to have snapped out of it and looked to Benny for answers.

"He's Red," Benny whispered to her.

"Bendy, me not liking this blood."

"I know, buddy. It will be gone in just a few more minutes. Can you hold this on your nose?"

"Me can."

"Thanks. Have a seat and I'll be right back."

Uncle Karl sat in the bean bag chair on the floor and Benny motioned with his head for the girls to follow him outside.

Angel asked, "What the hell was going on in there?" It looked like you were going to kill him!"

"It wasn't what it looked like. When I got here he was acting like me and he confronted me and attacked."

"He's getting worse," Nina said. "He seems to be switching more often now than he ever has. When it started he was switching every few weeks. Now he seems to switch every few days."

"Has he been taking his meds?" Benny asked.

"I don't know," Nina confessed. "Ever since the first murder happened I haven't slept well. And now that I have a real opportunity to make some

139

money with this interest in Tilley's local art, all I do is work in the studio."

"Is that why you're making the piece I saw on the floor with the numbers? Trying to capitalize on the ones from the murder scenes?"

"Yes, and I'm not ashamed to say it either." Nina's face began turning red and her breathing quickened. "You've been in the house. You've seen what a disgrace it is—maybe I could make enough to get a new roof. Maybe I could make enough to fix up a room or two and at least begin to repair the last thing my family owns. Now if you'll excuse me, I have a painting to finish." Nina stomped back into the house.

"I'm sorry you had to see that," Angel said.

"I probably deserved it. I beat up your Uncle and put your mother on my list of murder suspects."

Angel laughed. "I guess you do deserve it. I've actually been in charge of making sure Uncle Karl takes his medications. You have to trick him into taking them. I tried getting the ice cream truck driver to put it in his ice cream every day, but I don't think he understood what I was asking. He just kept talking about a Camero and asking for my phone number."

"Yeah, I spoke to him earlier and I don't think he would be able to handle that."

Uncle Karl came out the studio door and handed Angel the bloodied washcloth. "Must have spilled some red paint," he said, handing it to Angel.

"You must have."

"I think I'm getting a headache." He rubbed his forehead and the bridge of his nose.

"Do you want me to get you something for that?"

"Oh no. I know your tricks. You'll pretend it's headache medicine and it'll really be that medicine Dr. Walton wants me to take."

"And tell me again why you don't like to take it?"

"It takes away my creativity."

Benny tried to hide his laugh, but his cheeks puffed and gave him away.

"What?" Uncle Karl asked. "An artist lives through his creativity."

"I think you would be extremely creative either way," Benny said. "But let's get to what I came here for and I'll be on my way."

Angel started to turn to go into the house.

"Angel," Benny called. "I'd like to ask you too if you don't mind."

"Sure. I probably should check on Mother in a minute."

"Of course. But while you're here, what do you know about Erick Frederickson?"

"Little E?" Angel asked.

"Yeah, that's him."

"I've heard lots about him, but I've never met him. Growing up in Tilley it would be hard not to have heard some of the stories about him. It's been a while since I heard one though."

"Thanks, Angel. Why don't you go check on your mother now."

Angel turned to go and stopped. "Do you think you could just forget about her little outburst?

I still think the two of you might hit it off under different circumstances."

"Sure," Benny said. "Consider it already forgotten."

Benny turned his attention to Uncle Karl and immediately noticed fear in his eyes.

"Is he coming back? I don't have any money. I don't. I swear I don't."

"He's not coming back. He's dead."

Benny tried to gauge Uncle Karl's reaction.

"Really?"

"Really."

Benny saw relief.

"Why don't we go inside the studio and let me ride that horse of yours again and you can tell me all about him."

"OK. Can I wear the cowboy hat, though?"

"I guess so."

Chapter 16

Benny's houseboat looked as though it had been decorated like the most luxurious of homes. Nothing about it besides the slight swaying said boat. Even before he sold his house to Red, when he claimed he only used the houseboat as his office, the designer bed and his favorite pillow told a different story.

Benny tossed his keys on the kitchen island and pulled open one of the doors on the giant fridge. He smiled as he remembered one of the first times Rachael had been on the boat. She had puzzled over how large the refrigerator was and how he'd managed to get it through the door. He looked up at the skylight he had installed after the hole had been cut in the roof to drop in the giant cooler. He tried to forget the thought and grabbed a beer.

With one tilt he finished half the bottle and breathed out a sigh consisting of four stressful days. Once again he was back in the game he came to Tilley to disappear from—and he liked it. Faces and names and places swam around his brain as he tried to put all the pieces together. Benny felt the tingle, the rush, and he rolled his neck as the tension popped and cracked.

Benny spied the answering machine and noticed the flashing red light, signaling a new message. His heart hoped it would be Rachael, but his mind told him it wasn't. She was gone.

And he was wrong. It was her.

"Benny," she began, "I made the biggest mistake of my life leaving you. I may have made the second biggest mistake of my life by quitting my job this morning, but I did. I'm coming home on the next flight and I'm going to beg you to take me back. If you don't, I'll understand, but at least I'll have tried." She started crying and hung up.

Benny hadn't moved since the first whisper of her voice. In disbelief he reached out his hand and pushed the play button again. This time as he listened, he laughed and danced in place.

When the message ended he flew out the door and up the dock toward the office to tell Donny. He needed to celebrate and knew Donny would be just the one to feel his elation.

Benny busted in the door. Donny had his head in the bait refrigerator counting worms.

"She's coming home!" Benny screamed.

Donny popped up and smacked his head on the top of the fridge.

"What? Tell me you ain't kidding?"

"She quit. Rachael's coming home!"

Donny screamed like he had just won the largest lottery jackpot in state history. "She loves us! She loves us!" Donny began a happy dance the likes of which Benny had never seen. Benny began a dance of his own as Donny came around the counter still dancing and jumped into Benny's arms. Tears poured from Donny's eyes as he trembled and Benny just laughed and laughed.

"That's what happens when you come to this town," Donny said rubbing the top of his head. "You can't forget us. We crawl right up under your skin and stay whether we're wanted or not."

Benny shook his head and said, "You think she might be coming back for me?"

Donny looked perplexed. He scratched his head as though he were deep in thought. Finally he began bobbing his head up and down as he said, "Maybe."

"I'm going back to the boat and I'm going to try to call her back."

"Tell her I said to hurry."

"I will."

As Benny emerged from the office the evening looked different. The setting sun had more colors than before. The air smelled sweeter, and felt warmer. There was a buzz in the air that had not been there before. He felt like a school boy, in love for the first time.

As he neared his houseboat he noticed the door was open. He didn't remember leaving it open but didn't remember closing it either. He noticed a speedboat travelling faster than allowed out of the marina and he knew something was wrong.

Picking up a wooden oar from the dock, he inched toward his boat and listened. Aside from the motorboat speeding off into the distance, there weren't any other sounds. Peeking his head into the doorway of his home, Benny didn't immediately notice anything awry. The door to his bedroom was closed, and he knew for a fact he always left the door open to let air circulate. Carefully, he opened the bedroom door, readied with the oar to strike. He at least expected to find another piece of twisted art. Nothing. He checked the bathroom. Nothing. The closets. Nothing. And even strange places like inside the fridge and oven. Nothing.

Taking the oar back outside and putting it back where he found it, Benny decided it must have just been his overexcited imagination. He decided he had left the door to the houseboat open and for some reason shut the door to his bedroom. And the boat speeding away, ignoring the no wake rule, was just a coincidence.

Benny's thoughts slipped back to Rachael and he picked up the phone to tell Vernon the good news.

"Why don't I come by for a quick beer to celebrate?" Vernon suggested. "I'm just around the corner."

"Sounds good. That'll give me a chance to tell you about my visit to the Oglethorpe place today."

A few minutes later Vernon arrived and the two men clinked glass beer bottles together.

"She couldn't live without you, huh?"

"She sounded pretty homesick. I hope she doesn't regret her decision and in the end regret me."

"Nah. She's a smart girl. Maybe she made one bad decision, but I don't see her making two in a row. She knows what she's doing."

"I certainly hope so. Do you want to go up on the top deck and talk?"

"You inviting me to watch the sunset with you?" Vernon teased. "Gotta practice your romantic moves with lover girl on her way home."

"Very funny. If you're lucky I won't throw you off."

Benny led the way out the back sliding door and up the stairwell to the top deck. The sun had just slipped behind what looked like a small mountain of pines. Orange glowed atop the pines and hugged the water curling around the cove. It changed with every blink of the eye and for a moment the two were silent.

"I hear the sun rising is just as pretty," Benny said.

"Don't see that one too often, do you?"

"Nope."

"I see why you like it out here so much, though. The ripples on the water don't even look real. Some are going that way and others are going that way and somehow it all seems to be in synch."

"It never gets old. That's for sure."

"Tell me about the Oglethorpe's."

"Well, it all started today at Red's place. I woke up almost early enough to catch the sunrise. I was worrying. I called Red because he somehow always makes me feel better no matter what is going on. He told me Uncle Karl had someone coming by who talked funny."

"As in stutters?"

"You guessed it. I stopped by the station to pick up a picture of Little E to show Red, but Officer Mandelino was the only person there. I actually tried to call you this morning, but you didn't answer."

"I actually slept in. Walking around last night kept me up until three or so."

"I showed Red the photo and he says it's the guy who's been coming by and asking Uncle Karl for money."

"Oh, damn," Vernon said. "This is all making my head hurt."

"Tell me about it."

Benny ran down below to get two more beers and proceeded to tell Vernon about Uncle Karl pretending to be him and then Red, and then turning back into himself again.

"So what did he say when you got him alone again?"

"It wasn't really what he said. It was what he did that blew my mind."

"Which was?" Vernon coaxed.

"So there I was rocking back and forth on a wooden rocking horse, talking to a man in a cowboy hat sitting in a purple bean bag chair."

"Quite a picture."

"I don't know where the idea came from, but I pointed my hand at him like it was a gun and told him that I challenged him to a duel."

"You did what?"

"A painting duel. He accepted and got out two fresh canvases. Mine took me about forty-five minutes and his took six hours. He won." Benny took a deep pull from his bottle of beer. "Remember when I told you that Nina told me Uncle Karl really couldn't paint? That he was just pretending to be an artist?"

"Yeah."

"He can paint. He painted one of the best, most extraordinary pictures that I have ever seen. It had layers upon layers of paint. It was as though he would paint an entire picture and then paint another one on top of it. When I was finished with mine I sat back in the purple bean bag chair and watched in absolute amazement the entire time. In the six hours that I watched, at no point was I bored or wished that he would hurry up and finish. It was a show like I have never seen and I'll remember it my entire life."

"Now my head hurts even more. Why would Nina tell you that he can't paint?"

"I don't know. Maybe she doesn't know. Maybe she didn't want us to know for some reason. I really have no idea."

"What's that shining in the water?" Vernon asked.

"Probably the moon."

Vernon peered over the side of the boat and studied the lake.

"No, it's an inner tube you got tied to the back of your boat. Is that really where you were all day, floating around on your inner tube?"

"I don't own an inner tube," Benny protested.

"Well, then explain to me why a man who doesn't own an inner tube has one tied up to the back of his houseboat?"

Benny's mind reeled to earlier when he had thought someone had intruded into his space. He immediately knew the two were connected.

"Let me get my flashlight," Benny said rushing below. "Don't touch it in case it's rigged."

Benny flew down the steps and was back up before Vernon could even collect his thoughts.

"Shine it on what you saw," Benny said, handing the flashlight to Vernon.

Vernon pointed the light on the floating inner tube and said, "There it is."

Both men looked below and saw a painting sitting snugly inside a black inner tube.

"I'll be damned," Benny said.

"I don't think it's booby trapped. Let's go get it."

"OK." He felt duped for not looking around the outside of the boat after he felt invaded. He was glad that his senses were still intact, but felt let down by his lack of thoroughness.

Benny and Vernon made their way to the back of the boat. Vernon held the light above his head, shining it down on the water below, and Benny shuffled close behind him. Once at the stern, they could clearly see where the line was tied to the boat, which was holding the inner tube. Benny leaned over and grabbed it, and began pulling it toward him.

Once the inner tube was near, Vernon yelled, "Stop!"

Benny stopped pulling the line and Vernon inspected it carefully. He passed the beam over every inch of the floating tube.

"Pull it all the way in," he said, when he felt sure there was nothing that would explode or harm them in any way.

Vernon pulled two pairs of examination gloves out of his jacket pocket and handed one pair to Benny. He gently lifted the painting out of the inner tube and passed it to Benny. Bending over,

Vernon grabbed the inner tube and pulled it out of the water and set it on the deck.

"Maybe we can get some prints off the tube," Vernon said.

"Maybe, but I doubt it. Let's go inside and take a look at this painting."

Vernon followed Benny inside. Benny propped the painting on the counter and leaned it against the kitchen cabinets. He stepped back.

"No numbers," Benny said.

"This one is definitely different. Beautiful, really."

The painting was of a ballerina. She was on point, with one leg and both arms stretched out. Her head was pointed up toward an unseen light source, and her eyes were shut. She looked as though she was lost in her dance. The background was a blur of pinks and baby blues. There were no numbers on the canvas.

"That is amazing," Benny agreed. "Maybe there are numbers on the back."

He reached over and turned the painting around to find a single word written. It read, "Multiply."

"Multiply?" Benny said, turning the painting around again and stepping back. "Multiply what?"

"Multiply ballerinas?" Vernon tried.

"What about tutus? Ballerinas wear tutus. Could be two, twos which would be four?"

"But he's already used the number four. Tricky bastard. I figure he thinks we'll see the ballerina's tutu and make the connection and think four. What do you think?"

"I think you're right. We can keep it as our backup, but I think the number four is a wild goose chase this time."

"Then multiply what?" Vernon said aloud.

"Let's try something that I used to do with one of my old partners. For two minutes you'll think out loud and I'll listen. I won't be trying to figure this out at all—I'll just be listening, and then we'll switch roles."

"Can't hurt."

"Go."

"Pink, blue, smudged paint, dancing, closed eyes, heavenly, deep thoughts, balance, toes, arms out, lady, lady dancing..."

"Stop!"

"What?"

"Lady dancing."

"And..."

"Multiply it."

"Ladies dancing." Vernon thought. "Ladies dancing," he said again.

"Sing it," Benny instructed.

Vernon did as instructed. "Ladies dancing." He sang it again. And again. And it struck. His face lit up. Benny's face brightened.

Together they sang, "Nine ladies dancing."

"The twelve days of Christmas!" Vernon said. "Multiply one lady dancing and you get nine ladies dancing. Could it be?"

"I don't know," Benny said. "It's a hell of a stretch. Let's inspect the inner tube and see if it gives us any answers."

"If it doesn't, you have to come back in here and do that thinking out loud bullshit," Vernon laughed.

With their gloves still on, the two men each grabbed an end of the inner tube and brought it inside. Benny let Vernon hold it alone as he cleared the coffee table and asked Vernon to set it down. With the inner tube on the coffee table, they both fell silent and studied the black surface.

"I don't see anything," Vernon said. "I was hoping it would have something written on it."

"Me too. You would think it would have a number at least telling somebody how much to inflate it."

"Maybe it's on the bottom," Vernon said.

He grabbed the inner tube carefully and turned it over.

A nine volt battery was taped to the bottom.

Chapter 17

"Nine!" the two men screamed triumphantly.

"Son of a bitch," Vernon said. "It is nine ladies dancing."

"Nine," Benny said to no one. "Here we go again. What in town relates to the number nine?"

"Whatever it is, I imagine we got another dead body waiting for us."

"You can be sure of that. I guess my home is now a crime scene. Why don't you go ahead and make the call so I can get the boys in and out of here. I don't know when Rachael's going to be here and the last thing I need is a bunch of guys walking around dusting things and taking pictures. Nothing quite as romantic as a crime scene."

"When's she getting in?"

"I don't know. She didn't say if it would be today or tomorrow or if she was coming straight here or what."

"The crime scene guys are probably going to go over absolutely everything in this place. Have you bought anything special to cook that you put in the fridge? If so, you might want to go hide it at Donny's or something. You don't want them fingering all your food."

"I haven't had time to think that far ahead. She'll probably want to go eat at the little German restaurant in town. It was always her favorite."

Vernon's eyes doubled in size.

"What?"

"The German restaurant."

"What?" Benny asked again.

"That's where the dead body is. The German word for no sounds like nine—it's nein."

"Let's go," Benny said grabbing his keys. "Let your crime scene boys know the door is unlocked."

Benny drove.

Halfway there Vernon said, "You're awfully quiet."

Benny almost choked on his laugh. "Last time we were in a car together you yelled at me for talking while you were trying to think. Now I'm too quiet? I'm not so sure I need a woman back in my life when I have somebody like you who can make me feel bad about everything I do already."

Vernon lost it and snot flew out his nose he was laughing so hard. When he finally stopped he asked, "Do you happen to have a tissue?"

"Glove compartment."

Vernon opened it and pulled out a few napkins from a hamburger restaurant. He wiped his nose and the snot off the dashboard.

"You sure do like Wendy's," he said, admiring the stash of napkins. "And sorry about that. I'm just nervous. And I bet Rachael isn't one of those type of women you were joking about."

"She's not."

Benny pulled the Jeep into the gravel lot of the German restaurant. Being about dinner time the lot was fairly full.

"I don't get it," Vernon said. "Is there a dead body under the buffet table and nobody has seen it yet? How can there be a dead body inside a restaurant full of people that nobody has noticed?"

"I guess we'll find out."

Benny and Vernon walked in to find the dining room three-quarters full. The owner saw Benny and his face brightened.

"Mr. Benny," he said. "You no come to see me sometime soon."

"It's been awhile."

"Where you sweet young lady?"

"She's out of town," Benny said, not wanting to explain the situation. "I'm not here to eat tonight," Benny started. "Have you noticed anything unusual today?"

"Yes."

Benny waited for him to tell him what strange thing he had noticed but he didn't.

"What?"

"Just some kids."

"You've noticed some strange kids?"

"No, kids do some funny prank."

"What prank?"

"The kids, they cut off my lock on the outside freezer and put on another one lock."

"Let me get this straight. You have an outdoor freezer you keep a lock on."

"Yes."

"Your lock was cut off and another one is now on there?"

"Yes."

"OK. You just keep doing what you're doing here and I'll cut it off for you," Benny said, not wanting to frighten him with his suspicions.

"Thank you, Mr. Benny."

"I'll be back with Rachael soon."

"Very much the excellent!"

Benny walked back to his Jeep and opened the back where he kept a few tools, one of which happened to be a hack saw. He grabbed it with purpose and walked toward the freezer behind the restaurant.

"You ever cut one of these off?" he asked Vernon.

"No."

"It's not as easy as it looks. We'll have to take turns. You go first," he said, smiling and handing the saw to Vernon.

Vernon took the saw and began cutting. Before long he found a steady rhythm and beads of sweat appeared on his forehead. About five minutes later, with little progress, he passed the task to Benny and he spent some time with the saw.

The two men went back and forth for half an hour. Finally, the lock fell to the ground.

Vernon looked at Benny.

"You already know there's a dead body in there. Accept it. And let's move on with our work. We're not here to ooh and awe over death. We're here to catch a killer. The killer wants us to ooh and awe over his cleverness. We don't ooh. We don't ahh. We solve murders." Benny was breathing hard.

"OK. I'm with you," Vernon said. "Let's do it."

Benny pulled the freezer door open. Before the chill of the frozen air hit them they saw the body. Flat on its back, a person with a frozen towel over its face lay with arms stretched over its head. Frozen washcloths covered the hands. Additional frozen towels covered the body. A thin layer of ice had formed on all the fabric covering the victim. A

157

paintbrush with three notches cut into the handle rested on the chest.

"Hard to tell with all the frost and ice if this is even a man or a woman. He must have been wet when he was brought in here. How else would he have that much frost and ice on him?"

Vernon took a step forward and got down on one knee.

"There are some empty bottles of water under the left leg. Get down here and look," Vernon said.

Benny crept up to where Vernon knelt and got down on the freezer floor next to him.

"I'll be damned." Benny rubbed his fingers across the floor around the body. He did it on one side and then carefully leaned across the body and did the same thing on the other side. "I bet he brought the body in here, covered it with towels and washcloths and then poured water all over it to meld the body to the floor and to hide the identity."

"What is it with this guy and ice? The second body was in a cooler full of ice and now this."

"You got me. I guess we need to get this scene wrapped up before we go over my place."

"I was just thinking that. Could you stay with Red tonight or something? I can't see them getting over to your place for at least five or six hours."

"I'll call Carlton and see if I can get Rachael's old room booked at the Lakeside Motor Inn."

"Good idea. Why don't you go and tell the restaurant owner to clear the place out. We don't need everybody freaking out when the police cars and the coroner arrive. Tell him the department will pick up any money he loses tonight. It may soften the blow. Have him tell the customers we found a gas leak. They can find out the truth in tomorrow's paper."

"Good thinking."

Benny walked toward the back entrance of the restaurant, and Vernon pushed the freezer door closed as he pulled his phone out of his pocket.

Inside the restaurant Benny pulled the owner into his office and told him of his misfortune. He took the news fairly well and asked Benny to tell the patrons.

As Benny walked out of his office he noticed a stack of take-home containers and grabbed it. He walked to the center of the restaurant.

"Excuse me, ladies and gentlemen. There is nothing to worry about, and no reason to rush out of here, but we have just discovered a gas leak behind the building and for your safety I'm going to have to ask you to leave. There is no charge for your dinner. If you would like to put what you have not eaten in a take-home box please let me know and I will bring you one. Thank you all for understanding."

A few people raised their hands and Benny walked over to them and handed over a Styrofoam box as he thanked them for understanding. Others, almost finished, took one last bite and quietly stood up, conversing under their breaths with wide eyes. Before long the restaurant was empty.

Benny found a phone and called information for the number of the Lakeside Motor Inn. Carlton answered.

"Mr. Davis," Benny said with a smile in his voice. "I need a favor. I've got a bit of a situation on my hands, and I won't be able to stay at my place tonight. I was hoping to get the room Rachael stayed in when she was here."

"I'm sorry," Carlton said, with a playful tone in his voice. "Somebody just checked into that room."

"Of all the rotten luck."

"Not really," Carlton said, chuckling.

"What do you mean?"

"I imagine Rachael will let you share it with her."

Chapter 18

Benny dropped the phone. He ran back outside to the outdoor freezer where Vernon was waiting for his crew.

"I have to go."

"Is she here?"

"She is."

"Then go. We'll be fine here."

"You sure?"

"More than sure. Go."

Benny ran to the Jeep, hopped in and slammed the door. He pulled the key from his pocket and stopped just as he was about to jam it into the ignition. His brain went into overdrive.

She left me for a job. She ended us with a phone call. But people make mistakes. She made a mistake. Rachael made a mistake and realized it. Go.

Benny jammed the key into the ignition and cranked. As soon as the engine fired he was off. His heart pounded as the miles flew by.

A rental car was parked in front of Room 12. Benny parked the Jeep next to it and shut off the engine. As he tried to gather himself, the door opened and Rachael stood in the opening, unsure of herself.

Benny opened the door and climbed out of the vehicle.

"Welcome home," he said.

"Do you mean it?" She pulled her hand to her face to hide her trembling lip.

"Of course I do. Don't cry." Benny walked to her and they embraced. Rachael shook with nerves.

"How did you know I was here?"

"It's still a small town." They both smiled. "Aren't you going to invite me inside?"

"I wasn't sure where I stood with you."

"Let's go inside and figure it out."

Benny pushed the door to Room 12. It shut with a bang.

As they rested on the bed, both staring up at the ceiling exhausted from their reunion, Benny got Rachael up to speed on the new case.

"So, who do you have your money on at this point?" Rachael asked.

"I honestly don't know. I'm having a hard time nailing down a motive."

"Well, I've got my money on Big E. It seems a little too convenient that his brother is involved. And now that he's out of the picture he doesn't have to worry about splitting any family money with him. Sounds like he wasn't the sort of guy you would want around anyway, money or no money."

"Then why all the crazy art stuff?" Benny asked, playing devil's advocate.

"To throw everybody off. From what I understand, it seems like maybe he thought it would be easy to pin this all on Uncle Karl."

Benny laughed.

"What's so funny?"

"I was just laughing at myself—and you. I call a guy Uncle Karl who isn't really my uncle and it just sounded funny coming out of your mouth as well."

"What I don't understand though," Rachael said, pulling the sheet up under her chin, "is why the two other murders. If he wanted to get rid of his brother, that's one thing, but he took two other lives as well."

"Assuming it was Big E, he would almost have to take out at least one other person so it wouldn't look like it was all about his brother."

"That's a good point."

"We can dig a little more on him tomorrow. I have to check on the houseboat in the morning and then check in with Vernon to see if they got an ID on the body."

"Mind if I tag along?"

"I was hoping you would. We'll need to stop in to see Red, too. He'll be glad you're home."

"It does feel like home," Rachael said.

As Benny and Rachael walked out of Room 12 the following morning, Carlton was outside the lobby talking to a customer. He looked Benny's way and offered a wink that said more than any conversation could.

With Benny's focus directed at checking out the boat and getting on with the day, he forgot all about the obstacle of Donny seeing Rachael. When he did, it was too late, and he didn't have time to warn her how badly she had been missed.

Donny walked toward them on the dock and happened to be looking down at his sunburned feet. When he looked up, Rachael was a mere five feet from him. Startled and filled to the brim with joy all at once was too much of a shock for his body, and the jolt of electric feelings buckled his legs. Being a narrow dock his knees bounced just at the edge and he toppled into the water.

Coming up for air he splashed water on his face and said, "I've been baptized anew! The prodigal's daughter comes home."

Rachael smirked. "I'm glad to be home."

Donny splashed his face again and looked at Benny. "Did she say home?"

"She certainly did."

"Oh my," Donny said, pushing back from the wooden pier into the back stroke. He spit water out of his mouth and chuckled as he swam away from the dock.

"I think he's happy to see you."

"I would say so."

"We'll talk to you later, Donny. We have a busy morning."

"And I've got a hug for you when you're dried off," Rachael added.

Donny kicked his feet and spewed more water from his mouth.

The boat checked out and aside from a few items being out of their normal place, Benny could hardly tell that a crew had gone over it looking for evidence.

"They don't usually clean up this well. I feel special," he joked. "Why don't we get out of here before Donny finishes his swim. If he corners you now, we may be here for a long time."

A few minutes later they pulled into Red's driveway. Benny had called ahead, asking him to put on a pot of coffee and to get ready for a surprise.

Knocking on the front door, Benny heard Red call from inside to come in the house. He was sitting on the couch with his hands over his eyes. Rachael walked in behind Benny trying not to make a sound.

"Are you ready for a surprise?" Benny asked.

"Red know what it bees."

"Did somebody tell you?"

"No. Red just smell Rachael. I hope that good smell be her."

"It is me," Rachael announced.

Red pulled his hands away from his face and popped up off the couch. He gave her a gentle hug and as he stepped away, Benny could tell he was beginning to tear up.

"You really did miss her," Benny said.

"Red do miss her, but Red eyes showing that he heart be happy for Bendy. Bendy now can be all the way happy."

"I couldn't have said it better myself, buddy. We can't stay long, but do you want to have dinner with us one night this week?"

"Red liking that."

At the station, Vernon and Chief Neighbors were talking at the front desk when Benny and Rachael arrived. From the look on Vernon's face they both knew that whatever had been uncovered the night before and into the early morning was especially bad news.

Vernon and Chief Neighbors both gave Rachael hugs of welcome. Chief Neighbors' hands slipped a little past her lower back during his hug.

As Rachael backed away she slapped an open fist onto his chest.

"You haven't changed a bit, Charles."

"And don't you forget it," he said with a wink. "If you ever get tired of that old boy, I may be available."

"Can we get back to reality?" Benny asked. "I can tell by your faces that something more than just another dead body was found."

"Yeah," Vernon began, "unfortunately we know this one. When she thawed out, we were able to remove the frozen fabric from her face."

"She?" Benny said, gritting his teeth and taking a deep breath.

"Yeah. It was Hazel Walton, Dr. Walton's mother."

"I knew there was something fishy about her."

"The old lady?" Chief Neighbors asked.

"Yeah. I went over there a couple days ago to ask Dr. Walton about Karl Oglethorpe—I had his daughter's permission. While I was there his mother made us dinner and on the way out I saw a painting in her room made with numbers. She was real defensive about it. I would just about guarantee that it isn't there anymore."

"Dr. Walton made a positive ID on the body earlier this morning and I told him to expect a visit later today. Why don't you get on that Benny—see what he knows and while you're there you can see if the painting is still on the wall. If not, figure out how somebody would have gotten in there to get it and who that might be."

Rachael spied something interesting on Vernon's desk and her eyes began darting around the room.

"Why are all the phones off the hook?" she asked.

"They've been ringing non-stop all morning. Media."

"Word around town," Chief Neighbors said to Rachael, "is that you don't have a job right now."

"That's right."

"How would you like to be in charge of public relations for this case?"

Rachael smirked. "I do remember how terrified you are of the cameras."

"I am not!"

"Admit it and I'll do it for free."

"OK. Maybe I am."

"I'll do it," Rachael said as she began walking around the room hanging up the phones. Immediately they began ringing again and she yanked one off its receiver and put it to her ear.

"We'll be having a news conference at seven p.m." Benny heard her say as he waved to her and headed for the door.

Chapter 19

Dr. Walton had a hand-written sign on the door informing patients that the office was temporarily closed to observe a death in the family. A few people had left flowers.

Benny knocked softly and waited. Knowing the residence was upstairs he wondered if Dr. Walton could hear the door and tried the handle. It was unlocked. Benny stepped into the foyer and called, "Dr. Walton?"

"Upstairs," he heard him reply. "Please lock the door behind you. I'm not expecting any other visitors today."

Benny locked the door and climbed the wooden stairwell. Each step made a different sound, and the creaks reminded him of a horror film. That, combined with the stillness of the house, created a strange atmosphere that settled uncomfortably in Benny's chest. He was no stranger to death, but the familiarity didn't make it any easier.

Dr. Walton was sitting in the dark at the kitchen table with a cup of tea. His back was to Benny as he entered the room. Walking past him toward an empty chair he paused by the doctor's side and placed his hand on his shoulder.

"I'm so sorry for your loss." For all the times he had to deal with death and speak to family members, Benny had never thought of anything better to say. He knew there were no magic words and time was the only thing that would be able to ease a little of the pain.

"Thank you," Dr. Walton replied. "I'm still in quite a bit of shock."

"Of course you are. Be careful with the power you have of writing prescriptions to cover up the pain."

"I thought about it, but I know better."

"Good. You have to feel the pain at some point."

"I appreciate your honesty, Mr. James. I can tell you have sat at many tables like this one before, with people hurting in situations like my own."

"I have, but it doesn't make it any easier, and it doesn't make your situation any less important to me. I have found through my experience that a lot of people want to skirt reality in times like this and pretend that ugly things don't happen in this world. I've also found that people like yourself need honesty. You need reality. It's the best way for your mind to get through it."

"As strange as it sounds, it makes sense. I have had a patient for years I've been telling to get his torn rotator cuff operated on. He seems to think it's going to magically heal itself and he masks the pain with medications. If he would just face the facts that it's never going to heal itself, bite the bullet and get the surgery, he would be fine and pain free in no time."

"Exactly."

"I guess you need to ask me a slew of questions and take a look at Mother's room."

"I do."

"I'm ready," Dr. Walton said taking a sip of his tea.

169

"Did your mother have any known enemies?"

"No. The only person I have even seen her angry with in years was you."

"She *was* pretty perturbed about the painting. Why do you think she got so bent out of shape about that?"

"Oh, she and Karl Oglethorpe go way back. She knew him when he was, shall I say, a little more lucid than he is these days. Nothing romantic though. Just old friends."

"And do you still feel that he has absolutely nothing to do with the murders?"

"Positive."

"Do you have any theories about who would want to harm your mother?"

"No."

"Did Officer Kearns tell you about the painting connected to your mother's death?"

"No," Dr. Walton said, putting his tea cup on the saucer with a slight rattle.

Benny gave him the shortened version.

"Do you still think this has nothing to do with the painting in her room?"

"I seriously doubt it," Dr. Walton said, picking at his chin. "I think she was just in the wrong place at the wrong time."

"Is the painting still hanging above her bed?"

"I haven't been able to go in there today."

"Would you be willing to change your mind if it's gone?"

"Nobody has been in this house. I can attest to that. You saw, you can't get up those stairs without the whole house knowing about it."

"Let's have a look."

Benny stood. Dr. Walton pushed his hands against the table in getting up. He exhaled deeply as if every movement hurt.

The men stood before the door. Benny turned the knob and pushed the door open. As he suspected, the painting was gone.

Big E hid a key under a flower pot next to the front door. The same contractor who had renovated the house was sending over a trusted contact to repair the damaged door jamb and sheetrock caused by the dust-up with his brother.

He drove his golf cart down to the dock and boathouse below. The oversized boathouse held two high-end boats. He also had a smaller vessel tied to the dock. In all, he possessed twenty boats or more including speed boats, pontoon, fishing, and sailboats. Most of the boats were leased to patrons who kept them at his marina as it was a condition of the agreement. Big E did not want the boats to get too far out of his sight, and he rarely if ever sold a boat as he could not produce legitimate paperwork to accompany a sale. The computer age had made the business of stolen boats tricky.

Boats in Georgia contained two identifying numbers that were hard to fake. The HIN, or hull identification number was a number given to a boat upon manufacturing, which was registered with the United States Coast Guard. Usually, this number was stamped into the actual hull or a metal piece was riveted to the hull. Once a HIN is created, it is a rare occurrence for the number to be changed. The registration number, in the state of Georgia, is maintained by the Department of Natural Resources. With a little inside help, Big E could easily fake these, the most visible of the numbers.

Big E didn't necessarily need the income from the stolen boats, but once greed seeps into a man's heart, it sends constant messages to the brain, which cause it to crave more and more money. The whole operation started small as most do. Before his brother's last stint in prison, Little E needed money to settle a debt and sold his older brother his sailboat. Big E gave him the money and Little E promised paperwork he never produced. As the boat sat in a slip at the marina, a guy inquired about leasing the boat and the idea of leasing stolen boats was born.

When the operation started, Big E set his limit at five boats. He felt he could easily get away with five. The marina held four hundred boats, so five was nothing. Five turned into ten and ten turned into twenty. His contact at the Department of Natural Resources had just quit and his brother showing up had him feeling as if his life was unraveling. Big E was searching for a way to get rid of all the boats—fast.

The X-Sailence Marina was tucked into a series of coves. One of the coves held the covered slips. An adjacent cove held a marine repair shop and a boathouse that had the capacity of holding a fleet of boats wet or dry as they waited for repairs.

Big E had an enormous outside door to the boathouse rigged to act like your typical residential garage door. As he approached he picked up a remote, pointed it in the direction of the door, and mashed the button. With a groan of metal, the door shuddered and began to rise. The main mechanic, Paul, a friend and participant in the boat scheme was in the middle of an engine overhaul when Big E piloted his boat under the still rising door. Once under, he clicked the button again and the door reversed direction.

"We need to talk, Paul," he said, with fear in his voice. The boat was still in motion.

"Can it wait?" Paul looked at Big E. "I know, dumb question. I'll be there in just a second."

Paul put the tool he had been working with down and made a mental inventory of where he was in the engine tear down process. He pulled out a shop towel, which had been hanging from his pocket, and rubbed his fingers and the palms of each hand.

"What's on your mind, Ernest?" Paul had never called his boss by his moniker as it felt disrespectful to him.

"We have to get rid of all the stolen boats." Big E wiped his arm across his forehead.

"How? They all have leases."

"I don't know. That's what we have to figure out, but with Little E's death, I'm sure there will be some people sniffing around pretty soon."

"We don't have a paper trail for them to follow."

"I know that," Big E said, trying to catch his breath. "If the cops were here snooping around and they talked to anyone on one of our leases or happened to start running boat numbers, we would be royally screwed. To top it all off, our contact at the Department of Natural Resources quit."

"What?"

"Yeah. We're screwed. You need to figure out a way to systematically get those boats back without causing suspicion."

"We could vandalize some," Paul offered.

"Cops," Big E countered.

"Right," Paul said nodding his head. "You could put them all in legitimate boats."

"That would cost me a fortune and look a little suspicious if I suddenly bought twenty new boats. Let's do a recall."

"A recall?"

"I want all the leased boats in here by tomorrow afternoon. Make something up. We're doing a routine inspection of some sort."

"OK. I can do that no problem."

"Then we can lock this place up until we get the situation figured out."

"You need a hacker," Paul suggested.

"A what?"

"A hacker. Somebody who is a computer mastermind who could break into the Federal database and create twenty new HINs. If we had somebody who could do that—we would be free from all our worries."

"A hacker can do that?" Big E asked.

"If you know the right person."

Big E began to laugh. It was an evil laugh.

"I know the right person," he said. "I know the right person."

Chapter 20

After leaving Dr. Walton, Benny touched base by phone with Rachael and headed toward the Oglethorpe place yet again. Rachael had quickly relayed to him that the phone had been ringing non-stop all morning. She sounded excited and full of energy. Benny wondered when and if the jet lag would kick in and pull her down.

Benny was surprised to find two vans and a truck parked outside the Oglethorpe place. Men were scurrying around and Benny wondered what might be happening.

Upon exiting his car, a man crossed his path with a ladder over his head. Another man followed speaking in a tongue he was not familiar with. Behind him trailed another man that Benny stopped.

"What's going on here?"

"Hi," the man said, bobbing his head up and down.

The man tried to walk past Benny, but he put his hand on the man's shoulder and stopped him. "I asked you to tell me what is going on here," he tried again.

"Hi," the man said, again with a worried smile.

"Do you speak English?"

"Hi."

Benny threw his thumb over his shoulder telling the man to get out of his face. As the man scurried off he said "hi" again. Benny couldn't help but laugh. He yelled "hi" back.

As he approached the front door, Angel stepped outside.

"Hi, Mr. James."

"Hi," Benny said, laughing again.

Angel was confused with his laughter.

"What's so funny?" she asked.

"Oh, nothing and everything," Benny answered.

"OK."

What's going on here?" Benny asked.

"Mom finally found enough money to get the roof fixed."

"That's great. What are you going to do with all those extra buckets that you won't need inside anymore?"

"Would you like to buy one or ten?" she joked.

"It will be a good problem to have," Benny assured.

"Maybe we can finally get this place back to a respectable level. It used to be so beautiful. I can barely remember it. I was so young, but I do remember how it used to be. I've seen all the pictures and heard so many people talking about it for years. Did you ever see the house in its day?"

"I'm afraid not. I haven't been in town too long. I guess you could say I'm still a newbie. I've heard people talk about it though. It must have been magnificent."

"It was," Angel said, as her eyes glazed over. "And it will be like that again if Mom's paintings keep selling. It's going to be special again. Do you have a special place?"

"Actually, I do. The way your eyes were just sparkling a minute ago is how I feel about my houseboat. I've made it my little slice of heaven and I don't know what I would do without it."

"I'm glad you have a place like that," Angel said, slipping back into her dreamy thoughts.

"I need to speak with your mother. Is she available?"

"She's in her studio."

"Is it all right if I go back there?"

"Are you here to tell her your old girlfriend is back in town?"

Benny's eyebrows shot up.

Angel noticed his surprise and laughed. "It's a small town. People at the café were talking about it last night. A cab driver told the guy at the McDonalds drive-through who told one of the customers who told somebody who came in to Rene's. You know how small towns work."

"But..."

Angel cut Benny off before he could get his thought out. "I know you two never actually had a relationship, but the possibility of one was there."

"OK," Benny said, still lost.

"I know it's hard to explain to someone without an artistic mind, but possibilities sometimes feel like realities to artistic types."

"OK," Benny said. "I can go with that. 'Possibilities are sort of like realities.'"

"Thanks," Angel said. "Let her down easy."

Benny knocked softly on the studio door.

"It's open," he heard.

Benny pulled the door open. The bright lights from the studio hit his face and the warmth from the massive lights penetrated his cheeks. For a moment he felt a wave of uneasiness pass through his head. He took a deep breath and walked forward. The center of the studio was a safer place from the harsh lights. He found a spot he was comfortable with and stood still, examining the rest of the room. He still had not seen Nina.

"Nina?"

"Over here," she answered, barely audible.

She stood behind an Oriental partition. Benny walked across the room and around the partial wall. Nina stared blankly out the window. She bit her lip.

"I guess you found out the truth," she said.

Not sure which truth she was talking about, Benny answered "Yes," and hoped for more. Luckily, she had held in her secret too long and she spilled.

"It all started innocently. Before the house began to fall apart we used to have a spectacular art collection. Little by little we have had to sell it to stay afloat, but like I said, at one time it was grand." Nina smiled remembering. "From time to time, we would allow magazines and such to come and see our collection. Our collection has been in at least a half dozen magazines or more. On one of those occasions an art critic I had admired for years and years came to the house. Karl, without me knowing, hung one of his paintings in a hallway toward the back of the house. I was giving the critic the tour and when we walked past it he happened to be walking in front of me. He stopped dead when he got to it. And he loved it. He went on and on about how wonderful it was."

"And you told him it was yours."

"I told him it was mine. Of course he wanted to see more. I showed him a few paintings that really were mine and could tell he wasn't impressed. So I hurried out to Karl's studio and grabbed a few of his canvases. Again, he loved them."

"Did Uncle Karl ever know?"

"He never said he knew, but it kind of became a kind of unspoken thing. He and Angel just played along with poor Nina."

"I like your work."

Nina's face didn't change.

"Big E likes your work," he tried again.

Nina huffed. "He just bought that because he was trying to get into my pants."

"He has it hanging in his house in a pretty prevalent spot."

"He does?"

"He sure does. I'd say from where it hangs in his house that it's his favorite."

Nina's face eased. "Do you think I'm a horrible person?"

"No. I think you're human."

"Thank you."

"Can we talk about something else that might not be such an easy subject for either of us?" Benny asked.

"We don't have to," Nina answered. "I already heard that she's back in town."

"Oh. Yes, she is."

"If she hadn't come home do you think something might have happened between us?" Nina asked, turning red.

"It was a definite possibility."

Benny touched her lightly on the shoulder.

"Will you still help me with something," he asked.

"What?"

"I would like you to meet me down at the station tomorrow to look at the paintings we found that are connected to the murders. I want you to look at them and tell me if you know who did them."

"OK."

"Do you think you'll be able to tell?"

"If I know the artist who did them, I'll be able to tell. I have an eye for it. You can count on that."

"Thanks. I'm going to stop in to see Uncle Karl on my way out."

"Good luck with that. He's in a really bad mood today. The ice cream truck didn't come this morning."

"Uh oh," Benny said, leaving the room.

As Benny walked toward the front door he could hear footsteps scurrying around overhead. Dust floated in the air and he noticed small pieces of debris and paint peelings on the battered hardwood. He wondered what the roofers were going to find when they ripped off the shingles.

"You think they're going to fall through?" Angel asked, startling him.

"I was just wondering that. I hope your mom has enough money. I have a feeling the roofers are going to have to replace a lot more than just shingles. I bet a lot of the boards under there are rotten too."

"She does. Did she tell you the good news?"

Benny wanted to answer yes in case he said no and she wouldn't tell him.

"Well, she won't mind me telling you. She sold a giant stack of canvases. Cash. I bet she had fifteen thousand dollars in her purse yesterday."

"That's great!"

"Yeah, and she's rounding up some more today and painting more as fast as she can. Maybe we can finally get this place back to the way it used to be."

"That would be nice. I'm going to pay a visit to Uncle Karl before I head out."

"I wouldn't do that," Angel warned.

"I already heard that the ice cream truck didn't come this morning and he's in a pretty foul mood."

"You've been warned."

Benny knocked on Uncle Karl's studio door.

"What?" Uncle Karl screamed.

Benny opened the door and peeked inside.

"It's your friend, Benny."

"Nobody's my friend today. How can a man be pleasant when he didn't have any ice cream for breakfast?"

"I somehow do it every day."

"I'm not in the mood for your funny business." Uncle Karl spit on the ground.

"Can I ask why he didn't come?"

"Suspended."

"He got suspended from school?"

"Are you dense?"

"I guess so. Explain it to me."

"The ice cream truck has a giant cooler on it that gets filled up with drinks every morning. It's the biggest cooler you've ever seen. I bet I could get in there and take a nap."

Benny's eyes widened and he tried to hide his increased interest in the topic.

"I love naps," Uncle Karl said. A pleasant air began to descend upon him before he remembered he was too angry to be filled with happy thoughts. He kicked a metal stool that screeched across the hard floor and toppled over. "But then you wake up and you don't know if it's morning or night or what day is."

"Can we get back to the cooler you were telling me about? What happened to it?"

"It got stolen off the truck. Big E thinks the kid had something to do with it. Like he sold it or something. Nobody wants the job so he didn't want to fire him. So he suspended him for two days trying to show the kid who's the boss."

Benny knew he shouldn't have, but he asked, "I thought you owned the truck?"

"Well, well, Big E's the manager and I have to stand behind my people." Uncle Karl's eyes danced back and forth in his head.

"That makes sense," Benny lied. "Who do you think stole the cooler?"

"Probably a fisherman or a hunter. But I'm too mad to talk about it."

"Do you know where the kid lives?"

"I'm too mad to talk any more today."

"I'll take you into town and buy you as much ice cream as you want if you can show me where he lives."

"Let's go. I'm talking again." The pleasant air that a moment before had been chased away came back in an instant and splashed across Uncle Karl's face.

Benny wondered if Uncle Karl was going to hang his head out the car window like a dog.

Chapter 21

As Ned read through the notebook he'd been keeping on his pain threshold experiment he heard a car coming down the driveway. He assumed it was Benny and stuck the notebook under the couch. He didn't want Benny to get the idea he was thinking of restarting his study now that he was rested and feeling better. Ned felt as though he had learned a great deal about his body's tolerance, and it would be a shame if the information was all for nothing.

When the car stopped outside, Ned heard two doors shut and decided Red must have come along with Benny. When he heard the voices outside he knew it was neither of them.

Big E and Paul stepped over the two stairs leading to the front door and pounded. From the noise, Ned knew it was not going to be a friendly visit.

Ned began to pull on the door and just as he cracked it open the two men pushed him back into the room. As Big E continued walking, he forced Ned back into the house. Paul shut and locked the door.

In the living room Big E instructed Ned to sit. Ned sat.

"We hear you're a computer whiz," Big E started.

Ned had an idea.

"What?" Ned asked. "No, hello, thanks for inviting us into your home, what's your name?"

"You being smart with me?"

"Didn't you just say I was smart?" Ned said smiling. "No you didn't, you actually called me a whiz, so I guess I'm not being smart with you, I'm being a whiz with you."

"Does this guy know who you are?" Paul asked. "You want me to show him we're not here to mess around?"

"Is your girlfriend going to hit me?" Ned said waving his fingers at Paul with a provocative gesture.

Big E backhanded Ned across the face. "No, I am."

Ned tried not to show his pleasure with the situation.

"You have meaty hands. Kind of felt like I was just hit with a ham. I've never actually been hit with a ham, but I bet if feels a lot like your meaty hands."

Big E and Paul looked at each other quizzically.

"You sure we got the right guy?" Paul asked Big E.

"Yeah, this is the right guy. He must be trying some sort of reverse psychology or mind tricks on us or something."

"He doesn't even know what we want."

"What do you bitches want?"

Big E sucker punched him in the nose. Blood started in a steady stream over Ned's lip, down his chin, and into his lap.

"We need a favor."

"Well when you ask so nicely, how could I refuse?"

Big E pulled his hand back again and Ned winced.

"I think he's starting to get the message," Paul said.

"No," Ned said. "I've just sworn off pork, so I don't want ham-hands to put his swine laden hands near my mouth again."

Big E kicked him in the shin.

"That's better," Ned gasped as he bent over in pain.

Big E tossed a list of numbers into Ned's lap.

"Here's what you're going to do for me."

"What makes you think I'd do anything for you sweethearts?"

Big E pulled his arm back. Paul stopped him.

"Tell him about the money," Paul said.

"If you can get these numbers changed so they're legitimate, I'll pay you twenty-five thousand dollars."

"What kind of numbers are they?" Ned asked.

"Hull identification numbers."

"Stolen boats, huh?" Ned asked.

"Let's just say they've been misplaced. Can you get into state and federal databases?"

"Does the Pope wear a funny hat?"

"Then I'll leave the details up to you to figure out."

"What makes you think I won't go to the cops?"

Big E reached inside his jacket and pulled out a gun. He placed the barrel against Ned's forehead and pulled the trigger.

"Because if I ever do that again, I swear to God the gun will have bullets in it."

"You've made your point loud and clear."

Big E noticed the laptop that Benny had dropped off for Ned sitting on a table. He balled his fist and hammered it in the middle. The top cracked, a table leg broke, and the laptop hit the ground as the keyboard spit letters across the floor.

Big E and Paul let themselves out.

As soon as Ned heard the car pull away he looked down at the pool of urine at his feet. His legs shook as he bent over and pulled his notebook out from under the couch. With a trembling hand he began making annotations.

Uncle Karl pointed the way to the house where the kid who drove the ice cream truck lived. He had an ice cream treat in each hand, and Benny had promised him he would stop by another gas station on the way home to get him two more.

The kid's Camaro was parked in the driveway. Benny patted his pants pocket. Benny had stopped by the bank and withdrew enough cash for the kid to make one Camaro payment with a little left over. He was ready to call in his favor.

The kid's mother sat in the empty carport smoking a cigarette.

"Good morning," Benny said, approaching. Uncle Karl had asked to stay in the Jeep so he could listen to the static in between the radio stations. He said he sometimes heard instructions through the noise. Benny didn't ask what kind of instructions he heard nor did he care.

"Ah Jesus and Mary," the mother said. "What did he do now?"

"He didn't do anything."

"You look like a cop or something. Am I wrong?"

"I'm a private detective working with the Tilley Police Department."

"So he did do something wrong," she said, extinguishing one cigarette and lighting another.

"No. I just need to ask him a few questions about a cooler that was stolen off the ice cream truck. It should only take a few minutes."

"He's in his room, back of the house." The kid's mother waved Benny inside.

Walking toward the back of the house Benny heard the kid's loud voice and stopped.

"Die you rat bastard! Take that! Die!"

Benny sprinted to the back and kicked the door open which had been cracked. The kid jumped out of his chair away from the door and toppled over a small table taking a lamp and a stack of compact discs with him to the floor.

Benny noticed he had been playing a shoot-'em-up video game.

"Whoops," Benny said. "They say those games aren't good for you, and I think we've just proved that here."

"What the hell?" the kid said, pulling himself up off the floor. "You scared the piss out of me."

"You were screaming 'die, take that, die,'" Benny tried.

"Yeah, it's called a video game."

"I didn't grow up with those. We played outside in the real world." Benny picked the lamp up and set it back on the table after he repositioned it. He tried to turn it on, but it didn't work. "I owe you one light bulb."

The kid restacked the compact discs. "I already told everybody that I didn't steal that stupid cooler."

"What makes you think I care about that?"

"You're a cop aren't you?"

"Sort of. Who told you that?"

"Angel Oglethorpe. She said you're investigating the murders in town and that you think her Uncle might be responsible."

"I don't think that anymore. I do want to hear what you know about the cooler being stolen."

"Why does everybody care so much about a stupid cooler?"

"Because whoever stole it, put a dead body in it and left it at a gas station in town." The details were being released later in the day to the media so Benny didn't mind dishing them out to the kid a few hours early. He watched for a reaction.

"Oh my God. It has my fingerprints on it. Am I going to be arrested?"

"Did you kill anybody?"

"No!"

"Then, no." Benny cupped his hands over his face and rolled his eyes. Benny dropped his hands. "Who do you think might have stolen the cooler?"

"I have no idea. Mr. Frederickson lets me park the truck here at night sometimes. And it was here the night the cooler was stolen. That is true."

"Do any of your friends know you park the truck here at night?"

"I have three friends and none of them would steal anything or kill somebody. No way."

"What about your customers? Do any of your customers know where you live?"

"No."

"You're lying."

"I'm not lying."

"I can prove that you are," Benny said.

"OK. Then prove it."

"Open the blinds and look out the window. Look at my Jeep and see who is in the passenger seat."

The kid walked across the room and pulled the string that raised the blinds.

"Oh yeah," he said seeing Uncle Karl. "Now I remember. I was sick one day a few weeks ago and his sister, Ms. Oglethorpe drove him over here because she said he was having a fit. I imagine he was pretty pissed this morning when I didn't show up."

"Yes he was. Can you think of any other customers who might know where you live?"

The kid thought.

"No," he finally said.

"Fine," Benny said pulling the envelope stuffed with cash out of his pocket. "I'm ready to call in that favor I asked you about earlier."

The kid eyed the full envelope.

"Is that really a full car payment?"

"And then some. Let's just say I'm replacing the light bulb I was responsible for breaking. You could probably make your car payment and buy fifty or sixty light bulbs with the remainder of the money."

The kid started to grab the money and stopped.

"What do I have to do?"

"All you have to do is make one phone call and tell a couple of harmless lies."

"I'll do it."

"I'm going to bring Uncle Karl home, and I'll be back this afternoon.

"I'll be ready."

Benny handed the kid the envelope.

Chapter 22

Benny met Rachael at Rene's for lunch. The place was hopping with media and locals as it had become the center point of the story. The walls were bare of the usual art as it had all been bought by various collectors and curious people wanting to cash in on the bizarre situation.

Rachael was greeted like a celebrity as she hugged and shook hands with a dozen or so people outside the café. The story had gained national attention. In similar fashion to the previous chapter in Tilley's notorious appearance on the national stage it was being followed like a soap opera. The various media outlets had sent their stars and Rachael knew them all. She made sure to tell them all about the news conference she had scheduled for seven o'clock.

Rene greeted them at the door. She was on high with the attention and the money that was pouring through the door.

"Welcome back, Rachael." Rene gave her a hug. "There's just something about this town that won't let you leave. I ditched Italy for this place."

"There certainly is. I think it's the people," Rachael said, pointing to Benny playfully.

"He's all right," Rene joked.

"A spot just opened by the front window," Rene said. "Are you expecting anybody else?"

"No," Benny answered. "It's just us. Is Angel working?"

"She is."

"I would like Rachael to meet her. Can she wait on us?"

"This is actually her table today."

"Perfect."

Benny and Rachael slid into the booth. He grabbed her hand across the table and squeezed.

"I'm so happy you're here."

"Me too. It feels right. London felt wrong from the start. I can't even begin to tell you where my head was."

"You don't have to," Benny said squeezing her hand once more and letting go.

"Thanks."

Angel approached their table.

"Hello." She placed menus in front of each of them.

"Hi, Angel," Benny said. "This is my friend, Rachael."

Rachael extended her hand and the two girls shook.

"I've seen you on television, and I hope you don't mind me saying so, but you're even prettier in person."

"Thank you, Angel. You wouldn't believe the amount of makeup I had to have on my face for television. It was ridiculous. I always felt so fake."

"Mr. James has been really nice to my family," Angel offered. "You're lucky to have him." Angel winked at Benny and he turned a slight shade of red.

"That's enough girl talk for now," Benny cut in. "You two can talk makeup and boys at another occasion."

The girls laughed.

"Why don't we start today with a couple of gin and tonics," Rachael suggested.

"As they say, it's five o'clock somewhere," Benny said giving a thumb's up.

"I'll be right back," Angel said.

"The phone has been ringing off the hook at the station," Rachael said.

"Any tips, or just media inquiries?"

"Mostly media. I did have a few angry women call for Charles."

"Did he hit on you this morning?"

"Of course he did!"

They both laughed as the drinks arrived.

"Are you guys ready to order?" Angel asked.

Benny and Rachael ordered and Angel disappeared again.

"I don't know how Charles keeps his job," Rachael said, taking a sip of her drink.

"Nobody runs against him. I've been putting a bug in Vernon's ear trying to get him to run in the next election."

"He's too loyal. He won't do it."

"And he's scared. He thinks the county would still vote by skin color."

"It's not 1950!"

"And you're not black. You don't know how he feels."

"I think African American is more appropriate."

Benny laughed. "I asked Vernon because I thought the same thing, and he said he didn't care. He said black was OK."

"Whatever. It's beside the point. He would make a great chief and sheriff. Tell me again how Charles is both Chief of Police and Sheriff of Gladdis County?"

"Gladdis County is the smallest county in the state of Georgia and Chuckie had the ingenious idea of combining the two positions to save the taxpayers money. They voted on it and it passed."

"That's right."

When the food arrived, the conversation paused.

As Angel walked away, Rachael's eyes lit up. "I have a great idea."

"Shoot," Benny said, as he tried to figure out a way to pick up his mammoth sandwich and sink his teeth into it.

"Instead of interviewing you tonight at the seven o'clock news conference, I'll interview Vernon. It'll be his coming out party. Once he's a star on the national stage, he'll be a shoo-in for Sheriff of Gladdis County."

"You think he can handle the pressure?"

"I guess we'll find out."

Benny and Rachael ate their lunch and chatted, catching up on random things that had happened in their lives since the last time they had seen each other.

As they were finishing their food, Benny noticed Dr. Walton entering the café. Benny was surprised to see Angel not only greeting him with a gregarious smile, but also a tight hug as she twisted him back and forth in her embrace. He beamed like a man without a care in the world.

"Did you see that?" Benny asked Rachael.

"Yeah. What did I just see?"

"Angel just hugged Dr. Walton. His mother was found dead last night."

"Then, why is he so happy?" Rachael asked.

"That's what I want to know."

Chapter 23

After a long lunch, Benny and Rachael split up again. She headed back to the police station to field more calls. She also wanted to break the news to Vernon that he would be going on television later in the day. Rachael hoped he would agree to the idea without seeing her and Benny's motives. They agreed he might balk at the idea if he knew the big picture.

Benny switched to iced tea and waited for the lunch rush to die as he pored over his thoughts and observed the room and all of its characters. His plan for the day was to eliminate at least a couple of suspects from his list. He decided to start with Rene. Benny felt that he knew her pretty well from all the lunches and drinks he had consumed in the past few years in her café, but he had hardly had any dealings with her away from her business.

Benny decided Rene had the most to gain monetarily from the murders, as she was getting a hefty cut of all the art sales. He wondered if her business was in some sort of financial jeopardy or if she had borrowed money to buy her boat and was having trouble paying it back. He made a mental note to go by Ned's when he left to get him digging into her bank records. Benny also remembered he had not picked up the laptop computer he'd dropped off a few days earlier.

Rene noticed Benny staring out the window deep in thought.

"Everything OK?" she asked quietly so as not to frighten him.

"We need to talk in private."

"Sure. Everything seems to be under control at the minute and I'm not expecting any more art to come in until this evening. We can go in my office and shut the door."

"That would be great."

Rene's office was small. It had four exposed brick walls, a desk, and two chairs. A painting of Venice and a calendar were the only two things hanging on the wall.

Rene did not walk to the other side of the desk and sit down, but pulled the two chairs apart and sat directly across from Benny.

She slapped his knee playfully and said, "Grill me. I'm ready." Rene gave him her best smile.

Benny was used to being the one that had the psychological advantage. He couldn't help noticing how she didn't separate herself from him with the desk, and how she was very much in his personal space.

Two can play this game. Benny scooted his chair a little closer to her.

"I feel like I've known you a long time," he began.

"You have. You moved to town right after I opened, so I guess you could say you've known me as long as anybody else in town."

"Tell me again why you moved here?"

"You know the story," Rene said, losing the smile. "What is this?"

"I know you were kidding when you told me to grill you, but I have to. So let's get it over with. Then we can go back to being friends. Let me do my job, and then you can hopefully forgive me for doing it thoroughly. If you didn't have anything to do with the murders we can both look back on this uncomfortable situation and laugh."

"OK. Do your job."

"Why did you move from Italy to Georgia?"

"My husband was transferred."

"Were you happy to leave Italy?"

"I was excited, yes. I had never been to the United States, and I was curious to see what life was like here."

"Were there any other reasons?"

"What kind of question is that?"

"Were you running away from anything? Was there anything or anybody you were happy to get far away from?"

"No! I don't have any enemies and I've never been in trouble with the law in this country or my own. I've never had a parking ticket or even a library fine."

"Why didn't you go back?"

Rene sighed. "I fell in love with this town and out of love with my husband. He worked constantly and I felt like the townspeople had become a family of sorts." She fidgeted and bit at her knuckle. "I don't see what any of my past has to do with the current murders."

"People kill for crazy reasons, and I've seen problems follow people across oceans before."

"I'm telling you the truth."

"You have lied to me before," Benny said, staring straight into her eyes.

"I never!" Rene said, standing up quickly and plopping back down.

"Think about it," Benny said, holding his gaze. "If it's the only lie you've ever told me you should be able to think of what I'm thinking about. I know what I know. If not, then we may have more problems to look into."

"Ah, Jesus," she said, as it hit her. "Big E."

"Bingo. Tell me about it."

"I didn't think you guys saw him leaving that day. I should have known you knew when you made that smartass comment about smelling cologne even though he doesn't wear any. You were already suspicious and testing me."

"Nature of the business. Now, spill."

"When my husband moved back to Italy I decided I wanted to live on a sailboat. I didn't need a big place and knew I would be working most of the time, so I went sailboat shopping. I was shocked at how much they cost. An acquaintance told me about Big E. The acquaintance said he had heard a few people leased boats from him. I drove over to the marina and he leased me a boat."

"Does he lease a lot of boats?"

"I don't really know."

"Go on." Benny scratched his forehead.

"When the lease paperwork was finished he asked me where I was going to keep the boat. I told him at either the Sleepy Cove Marina where you live or at his marina. I had hoped the Sleepy Cove Marina as it would've been closer to work, but that didn't work out. I thought it would cost fifty to a hundred bucks a month to keep a boat at a marina."

200

Benny tried not to smile but did anyway.

"As you know," Rene continued, "it can cost as much as a boat payment. I was floored. Big E knew he had me. I had just leased a boat and had nowhere to keep it." Rene paused. "What I'm about to tell you doesn't leave this room."

"Absolutely."

"Even to Vernon and Rachael."

"I promise," Benny said.

"Big E said something about being a busy man and not having time for a steady girlfriend and blah, blah, blah. What he basically offered me was a free slip for sex once a month. He calls it a date. I call it paying the rent."

Benny nodded.

"I know it's terrible and that's why I lied. I'm not the kind of person that lies or does horrible things. I just got caught in a really bad situation and made some bad choices."

"That's it?" Benny asked.

"I swear, that's it."

"Then we're done here."

They both let out sighs of relief. The stress that had filled the room dissipated.

"Aren't you going to ask me any more about the situation with Big E?"

"No. I don't think that has anything to do with the case—so that's a question that Benny your friend would have to ask you, not Benny the investigator."

Benny stood up.

"Will my friend please sit down for a second?"

"We're still friends?" Benny asked, raising his eyebrows.

"Of course. I understand you have an important job to do."

"Thanks."

"Do you think I'm a horrible person?"

Benny recalled it was the second time in less than twenty-four hours he had been asked the exact same question.

He gave the exact same answer. "No, I think you're human."

Benny called Vernon on his way back to the ice cream kid's house.

"I think Rene's clean," Benny said, when Vernon answered.

"I figured she would be, but you never know."

"She admitted that she had some dealings with Big E and explained why he was on her boat that day. I hope you don't mind but she asked me to keep it private."

"Hey, I don't care if it doesn't have anything to do with the case. If you're happy, I'm happy."

"That's what I like about you. I'm headed to see if I can eliminate another suspect. Remember all that mud we saw on the front of Big E's boat?"

"Yeah. We had talked about how he might've been the one who ran their boat into the shore at the first murder site."

"I'm going to try to shake some information out of him. What's on your docket for the next few hours?"

"Thanks to you, I'm about to have PR 101 with Rachael."

"You're welcome."

"I didn't say thank you."

"You'll thank me later."

"I doubt it."

"You'll be great—talk to you later."

Benny hung up and pulled into the kid's driveway. His mother was sitting in the carport smoking a cigarette.

"Is this all you do?" Benny joked, getting out of his car.

She didn't think it was funny.

"No. Sometimes I drink vodka while I smoke."

Benny wasn't sure if she was humoring him or not.

"I need to borrow your son, if that's OK."

"You can have him for all I care," she said, deadpan.

"I imagine he's shooting imaginary people in his room?"

She nodded as she took a drag on her cigarette.

Benny found the kid in his room doing just as he expected. Benny cleared his throat to announce his presence. The kid turned.

"You're not going to kick the door in this time?"

"Very funny. It's time to pay the piper, kid."

"Fine."

"Let's go for a ride. Bring your cell phone. The call needs to come from your phone. I'm sure he has caller ID."

Once inside the Jeep, Benny told the kid the rules.

"Here's how you earn the envelope full of cash I gave you," Benny started. "First of all, you will never, ever, speak of this to anyone. Not even me again. After you make the call and hang up, it never happened."

"You already paid me, and I already put the money in my bank account," the kid said, looking smug.

"How would you like to use that money to fix your broken windshield and your broken taillights? Maybe a slashed tire or two?"

"I don't have a broken... oh," the kid said catching on. "I won't say a word to anyone."

"Good, because I'm not kidding. You ever smashed a windshield out of a car with a baseball bat?"

"No."

"It feels so good. I've been looking for a reason to have that feeling again."

"I said I wouldn't talk about it."

"Perfect. Here's how the call is going to go," Benny said pulling the Jeep into a vacant lot and shutting off the engine."

He explained what he wanted to happen, trying to cover all the things that could possibly come up. The point he tried to drive home the hardest was for the kid to stay vague and let Big E do most of the talking.

The kid placed the call.

"What do you want?" Big E answered. "I told you that you could come back to work tomorrow."

"I just had a really weird visitor come to my house," the kid started.

"And why would I care?"

"It was an FBI agent and he was asking questions about you."

"What?"

The kid now had Big E's undivided attention.

"Yeah, I told you it was weird."

"What does this have to do with me?"

"He kept asking me about two things."

Benny gave the kid a signal to pause.

"What two things? What?" There was hysteria in his voice.

Benny nodded and held up one finger.

"First of all the guy kept asking me about the missing cooler. He said that a guy was found dead inside the cooler."

Big E didn't say anything.

"I passed a lie detector about it. I told them I didn't have anything to do with the missing cooler. I passed."

Benny gave the kid a gesture and a look saying he was off script. The kid gave him a little grin and a shrug of his own.

"Don't worry about the cooler. I guess you didn't have anything to do with it."

Benny noticed Big E didn't apologize. As Benny held his head close to the phone, almost head to head with the kid he could also tell by Big E's voice that the cooler issue wasn't striking a chord.

He held up two fingers signaling the kid to move on to the second topic they had previously discussed.

"The second thing they wanted to know about was your dirty boat."

"Oh, son of a ..." Big E's voice whimpered and trailed off. The kid had struck a chord.

The kid started to speak and Benny held his hand over the kid's mouth and shook his head back and forth.

"What do they know?" Big E pleaded.

"The guy just kept asking me if I knew anything about your dirty boat. It didn't make a whole lot of sense to me."

"What did you tell him?"

"I told him I didn't know anything about a dirty boat. What should I tell him if he comes back and asks again?"

Benny gave the kid a thumbs up.

"Did they say boat or boats? Think hard and try to remember."

Benny had a paper and pen ready. He quickly wrote boat on the paper.

"Boat."

"OK. Good." Benny heard relief in the two simple words.

"Thanks for the heads-up."

"You're welcome."

"Let me ask you one more thing," Big E said. "Did he say anything about a guy named Ned?"

Benny's eyes shot wide open.

Chapter 24

Chief Neighbors watched as Rachael put on makeup for the news conference. Vernon had gone home to take a shower and to change clothes.

"You're drooling, Charles," Rachael said, eyeing him in the mirror.

It wasn't a figure of speech. Chief Neighbors wiped away the moisture from under his lip.

"Sorry," he said.

"No you're not."

"Can I ask you for some advice?"

Rachael turned around. "That depends on if it's appropriate or not."

"It's appropriate," Chief Neighbors promised, "but you can't tell Benny or Vernon."

"This sounds like a slippery slope."

"I assure you it's not."

"How about we do this," Rachael suggested. "You start, and if you cross the line or begin to talk about anything that I won't be able to keep secret, I will tell you to stop."

"Fair enough. Jane called this morning."

"Jane as in your and Benny's ex-wife? That Jane?"

"Yeah. That Jane. She wants me back.

"Again?"

"Yeah."

"Hasn't she learned?"

"She's willing to give me one more chance."

Rachael turned back to the mirror, mascara pen in hand. She shot him a quizzical look. "Can you?"

"I do love her."

"That's not what I asked. Are you physically and mentally able to be with just one woman for the rest of your life?"

Chief Neighbors didn't answer the question. "She wants me to move to Arizona. She says I'd love it there."

Rachael turned around again. "Move?"

"Yeah. She thinks it would be good for me. I was born and raised in this town. The farthest I've ever been from here is Louisiana. She said I wouldn't have to work if I didn't want to and we could travel to all the places we talked about when we were young. She thinks that now we're older it might work."

Rachael wanted desperately to advise him to go. It would solve the problem of Vernon running against him in the next election, but her morals wouldn't allow her to do such a thing.

"I wish I could tell you what you want to hear," Rachael said, turning back to the mirror. "If I have to be deadly honest with you though, I'm going to have to say, from my vantage point it looks like it would be a mistake. I don't think you would be able to stay faithful, and haven't you already put that poor woman through enough?"

The Chief pulled at his mustache.

"When I left for that gig in London I was all messed up thinking of nothing more than my career. It only took me two days to realize once I was there that I had made the worst mistake of my life. It's not the money that matters in life. It's not the stature or the accolades. It's the people. Without the special people in your life none of it means anything."

"You may be right," Chief Neighbors said, as his eyes focused on the parking lot. "Vernon just pulled up." He walked toward the front window and peered outside. "Look at all the media vans out there. I dare say there might be more than the time I went on television with you." He paused as he remembered. "I was pretty amazing."

Rachael laughed at his lack of modesty. "You *were* pretty fantastic. Here comes Vernon. I hope you make the right decision about Jane. And don't worry; your secret is safe with me."

"Thanks. Should we hug it out?" Chief Neighbors asked with a suggestive wink.

"No, but nice try." Rachael gave him a wink of her own.

When Vernon walked in the door, Rachael knew instantly that the news conference and interview would be fine. She had been in the media business long enough to recognize the look of someone who was scared to death of the camera versus someone who was confident in their self and capable of ignoring the thought of hundreds of thousands of eyes upon them.

"You look great," Rachael said.

"I feel great. So how's this going to go?"

"We set up a podium outside like you would see at most normal news conferences. I also set up two chairs so we can sit and have an interview like I used to do on my show. I know it's not the way most news conferences go, but that's one of the things I like most about this town—you all don't always do things the normal way."

"You know you can start saying 'we' when you talk about Tilley."

"What do you mean?"

"You just said, '*you all* don't always do things the normal way.' You can start saying *we* don't always do things the normal way."

Rachael realized what Vernon was saying. "Thank you, Vernon. That means a lot to me." Rachael looked at her watch. "Five minutes and we need to get out there."

"When I was in town today I could tell people were pretty frightened. Don't you think this has the possibility of making it worse?"

"No. I guarantee that a lot of the information out there isn't true. It's our job to let people know the truth. If the truth is scary—so be it, but they have the right to know."

"I just don't want to make things harder on everybody by scaring them."

Chief Neighbors walked to Vernon and clapped him on the back. "You'll do fine. You're working with a real pro here," he said, nodding his head Rachael's way. "I was pretty nervous when I did the national TV show a few years back, but once we got going it was like it was just the two of us talking. She led me in all the right directions."

"Thanks, Charles," Rachael said, "and that's exactly what it is—just the two of us talking."

Rachael and Vernon simultaneously looked at their watches.

"You ready?" she asked.

"Let's do it."

Rachael walked to the podium at exactly seven o'clock. The media waited.

"Good evening ladies and gentlemen," she began. "I would like to thank each and every one of you for attending tonight and waiting patiently for the Tilley Police Department to formally address the situation. I would like to introduce myself and tell you my role in this matter. My name is Rachael Martin. In the past I have had the opportunity to work as a journalist for a few different networks. I may have had the pleasure of working with some of the people present here this evening. I have taken on a temporary role as public relations director for the Tilley Police Department."

Rachael paused momentarily for the information to be processed.

"This evening I am accompanied by Officer Vernon Kearns." Rachael looked at Vernon and he nodded. "Officer Kearns has been with the Tilley force for almost fifteen years. He has an exemplary record. You might remember reading about him during the last case that put Tilley, Georgia on the map, as he was an integral part of the investigation. Mr. Benny James has told me many times that the case may not have been solved if it weren't for the dedication and insight of Officer Kearns."

A local standing behind the hoard of media gave Vernon a rowdy rebel yell.

"Tilley, Georgia is not the kind of place where this sort of thing is supposed to happen. Life is slower in Tilley. People are friendlier. We do things different in Tilley, Georgia."

Rachael looked at Vernon and winked as she used the word "we."

"We're going to do this news conference differently too. I can guarantee that this is the first and will probably be the last news conference you attend that will be carried out in this fashion. I am going to interview Officer Kearns like I would have on my television show. Please welcome, Officer Vernon Kearns."

Rachael began clapping. The television crews, newspaper writers, radio people, bloggers, and all in attendance were not sure what to do as this was most definitely a first. The first claps came from the back. A few more scattered through the middle of the crowd and before long it grew into boisterous applause. Rachael and Vernon sat down.

"Thank you for agreeing to do this, Officer Kearns," Rachael began smiling deep into his eyes.

"It's my absolute pleasure. Thank you for asking."

"I would like to start by addressing the grave nature of the situation at hand. From speaking to you earlier I can tell you care deeply about all the people who live here."

"I do. I'm a police officer and protector, but I'm also more than that. People here call me friend and neighbor, and I don't like to see my friends and neighbors worried."

"Where are you in the investigation?"

"We're making progress every hour. I'm doing everything in my power to solve this case as fast as my department can so my friends and neighbors can get back to their normal lives. You mentioned Mr. Benny James earlier, the department has hired him to assist. I think most people know the experience he brings from the FBI. He has an incredible talent for solving tough crimes. As we speak he is following up on a lead we received earlier today."

"He said some very complimentary things about your talents earlier when we spoke."

"He's very kind."

"Let's get into the specifics of the case," Rachael suggested.

Vernon settled in and it was just as the Chief said it would be, just two people talking. And a couple million people watching on television. In Tilley and across the nation, Vernon had his coming out party.

Chapter 25

The next morning Rachael was gone when Benny woke at a few minutes after eight, which was a couple hours before he preferred. He was worried about Ned. He missed the previous evening's news conference trying to track him down.

Benny tried calling and calling without success, which wasn't weird, but the fact that he didn't answer the door was out of the ordinary. Benny even tried the side door and two back doors plus a window or two trying to get inside. Ned rarely if ever went anywhere. Although it was possible he was out, Benny doubted it and decided if Ned didn't answer the door on his next attempt he was going to kick it in and ask for forgiveness later.

As he drove toward Ned's, he had a great idea and called Red for a favor.

"Red here," he answered.

"Hey buddy. I need your help this morning."

"Sure, Bendy. Red helping with anything."

"Can you still climb like a Billy goat?"

"Oh sure. Red not even needing a ladder to get on you house."

"It's your house now, don't forget that."

"Right."

"I'll pick you up in a few minutes."

"OK. Red making you coffee."

Red met Benny in the driveway with a cup of coffee. Benny took it gratefully and thanked him for his thoughtfulness. Benny explained to Red what was going on and what he needed him to do.

The front door of Ned's house was locked once again. Ned was not a morning person, so Benny did not expect him to be awake. He did expect him to answer the knocking and the incessant ringing. He did not.

Benny nodded to Red and said, "Let's see your stuff, kid."

Red grabbed a column on the porch, put a foot up on the railing and launched himself upward. Standing on the railing he moved one hand to an old flag holder attached to the column. He pulled at it to test its strength. His other hand reached to the brick facade of the house and found a place to wedge his fingers into. He crouched momentarily and then in one fluid motion somehow jumped, pulled, and pushed his way onto the roof.

Benny walked into the yard where he could see him.

"How the hell did you do that?"

"Red not know."

"Start checking windows."

The second window he tried opened. He turned and beamed.

"Now do what I said so you don't scare the piss out of him and get shot or something."

"Ned!" Red screamed into the house. "Open you door or Red come in to open for you. Bendy very worry." Red listened. He yelled down to Benny, "He say Jesus Christ he coming." Red yelled back into the house, "It not Jesus Christ, it Bendy James."

Ned reluctantly pulled the door open. His nose was taped, lip split, and bruises were still forming on the left and right side of his face.

"My God," was all Benny could say.

Red appeared behind Benny.

"You not looky so good. Who bees mad at you?"

"Me," Benny answered. "I'm angry with him. Did you start that ridiculous research project again after it almost killed you last time?"

"Afraid so," Ned lied.

Benny walked into the house.

"Let me see you in good light so I can decide if I'm going to kill you or take you to a hospital. Get him some ice in a Ziploc bag or something," he instructed Red.

Red walked to the kitchen. A minute later he came back with a baggie of ice and a question. "Why you break you pewter, Ned. Is that what you fight about?"

Ned shook his head from side to side trying to tell Red to drop the subject. Red missed the communication.

"What are you talking about, Red?"

"They bees a pewter in he kitchen with all the alphabets around. Come look."

"Aw geez," Ned said.

Benny walked to the kitchen. Ned had put the broken laptop on the kitchen table. The keys from the keyboard were scattered around the table along with a few tools.

"This is interesting," Benny said. "Ned, my friend, you've got some explaining to do. Why is a piece of my evidence that I entrusted to you in shambles? I'm guessing you are lying to me about restarting your research and your face has something to do with this computer, but for the life of me I think it would take a million years or more for me to guess what. Why don't you end all of this suspense right now and tell me what is going on."

"OK. I was taking the computer downstairs to work on it. I moved my workstation for these type of things to the basement. As I was walking down the stairs I tripped and fell all the way down the stairs hitting my face several times and dropping and rolling over the computer."

"Fascinating," Benny said.

Red walked back into the living room and returned to the kitchen.

"Since you he friend, Red help Ned buying he a new couch."

Again, Ned shook his head back and forth to Red trying to tell him to stop. Again, Red missed it.

"Why is that, Red?" Benny asked.

"He missing one of he cushion and they some blood on side."

"Explain," Benny said to Ned.

"I..."

"Let me help," Benny offered. "Let's play a game."

"OK," Ned said, not sure where Benny was going with his thought process.

"I'll give you a word to start a sentence with and you say whatever comes to mind out loud."

"OK." Ned's bruised and battered face scrunched with confusion.

"Mushroom," Benny said.

"Mushrooms are delicious."

"You're very good at this game." Benny looked Ned in the eyes. "Round two." Benny paused. "Big E."

Ned's yellow and purple face turned red where it could.

"Big E is an unfamiliar term to me."

"Wrong."

"Big E is a person I have never met."

"Wrong."

"Big E will kill me if I tell."

"Ding, ding, ding. Although you are not entirely correct, you do win a prize."

"I hope it's Vicodin."

"No, it's protection until you decide to tell me the truth."

"I'll take it."

After gathering a few of Ned's belongings, Benny dropped them at Red's house. He promised to take good care of him and said he wouldn't let anyone know where he was.

Benny's next stop was the Oglethorpe place. He decided it was time for Nina to take a look at the art found at the murder scenes. He remembered her saying that if she knew the artist who had made a piece, she would be able to tell.

Heading down the long dirt drive, Benny's attention wandered from the road as he marveled at the metal sculptures off to the side. When he glanced back at the road, a car barreled toward him. The driver was trying to scrunch down in the seat and get out of sight. Benny slammed on his brakes and pulled off to the side to let the car pass. As the car passed he lifted himself as much as he could to get a better view and swore to himself that he recognized the driver. It was Dr. Walton.

The roofers were already set up and crawling all over the house. Benny wondered how long it would be until Uncle Karl started speaking Spanish and acting like some of the workers. He peeked into his studio. Uncle Karl was wearing a sombrero he had noticed in there on another occasion.

"*Buenos dias*," Benny joked.

"*Hola, amigo*," Uncle Karl answered. "Can you tell them to stop making all that doggone racket?"

"It's going to be awful hard for them to put a new roof on your house without making any noise."

"I don't go in there much anyways."

"Did I just see Dr. Walton leaving here?"

"Yes."

"I didn't know he made house calls?"

"He wasn't here to see me."

"Who was he here to see?"

"Ah, God. Do I have to tell this story again?" Benny's forehead wrinkled.

"Who did you already have to tell?"

"Clarice."

"Your ostrich?"

"Yes. She's the nosiest thing you've ever met. I just finished telling her why he was here."

"Be a pal and tell the story one more time," Benny said, climbing onto the rocking horse. "Do you mind?" he asked, pointing to the wooden horse under him.

"Nah, she hasn't been ridden in a while and could use a good workout. Warm her up slow."

Uncle Karl took off the sombrero and tossed it to his right without looking. This time he didn't knock off any jars, break, or spill anything.

"Dr. Walton was in love with Nina, but his mother didn't approve."

Uncle Karl started scratching his knee.

"That's it?"

"Yep."

"You were complaining about having to tell me one sentence? That's not a story. It's more like a fact or something."

"It's a short story."

"I'll say. Why didn't Hazel like Nina?"

"She thought Nina was after his money."

"Does Dr. Walton have a lot of money?"

"From what I hear he does. The family owns a prime piece of real estate in town. He's a doctor. What more do you want?"

"Fair enough."

Uncle Karl stood and walked over to one of his canvases propped against the wall. He picked it up and began to study it as if Benny was no longer in the room.

"I'll be going then." Uncle Karl turned to Benny, startled. "I'm going to take Nina into town to help me out with something. Is it OK with you if I ask her about her relationship with Dr. Walton?"

"Who told you about that?" Uncle Karl said running up to him. "Did Clarice blab all that to you? I told her to stop gossiping to strangers." He turned around and kicked the canvas he had been looking at. *"Que demonios es eso?"*

Benny shook his head as he left the studio.

Nina answered the front door.

"You got an hour to run up to the police station and look at the two paintings?"

"Sure, but I thought there were three?"

"One is a sculpture."

"I can't help you with that one—maybe Uncle Karl can."

In the Jeep on the way to the station, Benny questioned her about Uncle Karl.

"I talked with him this morning and he seemed somewhat normal. Then it was as if someone threw a light switch and he didn't remember talking to me."

"I wish I knew what to tell you. As soon as you think you've got him figured out he changes. Sometimes I think he does it on purpose, but I can't prove it—and why would somebody do stuff like that?"

"What does your doctor friend think?"

Nina blushed. "Did you see him leaving here a little while ago?"

"I did. I assumed he was making a house call, but Uncle Karl tells me different."

"Oh, God." Nina pulled her fingers to her flushed face. "I feel like a schoolgirl. I guess it's a good thing your girlfriend came back into town and nothing happened between us."

"I'm guessing so. We would've had one unhappy doctor on our hands." Benny pulled the car onto the main road off the long dirt driveway. "So, from your point of view, why didn't Hazel like you?"

"She knew we'd lost all our money, for one. She also thought my husband would come back one day and didn't want me breaking her son's heart."

"I guess I can understand that. Do you ever talk to your ex-husband?"

"Rarely. Maybe once every five years or so."

"Where does he live?"

"Small town in Tennessee."

"Does Angel ever see him?"

"She's mailed him a few things over the years, but he doesn't write back from either guilt or the booze. Maybe both."

"A real winner, huh?"

"Yeah. He's also never gotten over the fact that I went back to my maiden name and legally had Angel's name changed to Oglethorpe."

"What was it before?"

"Preston."

The conversation from this point shifted to lighter topics. Pulling into the police station parking lot, Benny had one last probing question.

"How much do you think you will have made selling your paintings when it's all said and done with what's happened in town?"

"Fifty thousand dollars."

"That's a lot of money for paintings."

"They see them more like investments. That's the sad part. Some people love art for the art and for others it's just another way to make some money."

Inside, Chief Neighbors and Rachael were talking. They stopped as Benny and Nina walked in the door.

"I need the key for the property room, Chief," Benny said, holding up his hand signaling for him to toss them.

Chief Neighbors grabbed at his belt and pulled out his giant ring of keys. He twisted the key to the property room off and tossed it across the counter.

Nina followed Benny to the door. He slid the key in the lock and the two entered. Benny turned on the light and shut the door behind them.

The room had a locker for the drugs with an extra lock attached. It also contained multiple shelves with white boxes, two tables, and a small closet. One of the tables held the metal sculpture found at the second crime scene, which happened to be the police department. They didn't have to transport it far.

"This is the sculpture we found. It had something else in it which has been removed, but it wasn't something made by an artist."

Nina stepped closer to it.

"Whoever did it can weld pretty well. They ran a very nice and steady bead where they joined these two pieces," she said, pointing without touching to an area of the metal. "This could have been a number of people. A good bit of the artists I know have a welder like the one used here and with a little practice, it's not too hard to run a smooth bead."

"Is Uncle Karl's welder the same type that was used to do this?"

"Yes."

Benny grabbed two latex gloves out of a box on the same table and put them on.

"I forgot to tell you. Don't touch anything. You don't want your finger prints on anything in this room."

He walked to the small closet and opened the door. The two canvases were the only thing inside. Benny pulled one out. He showed Nina the back side.

"Is this a normal canvas?"

"Yeah. It's not homemade or anything. Most of the artists I know stretch their own. This one is store bought and could've been bought at any art store."

Benny turned the canvas around so she could see the painting. Nina's face immediately went white.

Chapter 26

"I'm not feeling well," Nina said. "I... I think I may have eaten something bad this morning. I have to go."

She ran out of the room.

"I'll give you a ride home," Benny called after her. "Wait!"

He shut the door to the property room and walked back into the main area. The front door was already closing. Chief Neighbors and Rachael looked at Benny.

"I think she knows something."

"I have never seen a person throw up and run at the same time," Chief Neighbors said.

"She threw up?" Benny asked.

"Look at the damn floor all the way to the door."

Just as Chief Neighbors said the words the smell hit him and Benny spied the liquid droplets and chunks making a trail to the door.

"She said she felt like she may have eaten some bad food."

"Well, maybe she has food poisoning," Rachael suggested.

"I don't think so." Benny tossed the key back to Chief Neighbors. "I think she knows who painted that picture in there, and the information scrambled her brain and twisted her stomach."

"Are you going to chase after her?" Rachael asked.

"No. She can find a ride home or come back here and ask for one. I'll give her some time to process the information and get back with her tomorrow. Until then we need to get one of the deputies to watch her. Wherever she goes next may give us a good idea of who's behind this."

"I'll get Officer Mandelino on it right away," Chief Neighbors said.

"Where's Vernon?"

"He's running down some sort of lead he had on a boat. He said he checked a registration number and the results were fishy. He wouldn't tell me any more, which probably means he thinks it'll make me mad."

"I can assure you that it will," Benny said, bluntly.

"Ah, Jesus. Are you guys still picking on Big E? I'll be lucky if he sends me two dollars for my next election campaign after this."

"Maybe you shouldn't run again."

Chief Neighbors' mouth dropped.

"Why not?"

"You've been there and done that. I think at this point in your career that you are more suited to be a mayor, councilman, or maybe even a congressman."

"Really?"

"Yeah. For some reason people really like you." Benny gave him a playful wink. "And you don't like the blood and guts of the job. Mayor might be beneath you, but congressman would be right up your alley. Have you ever been to DC?"

"No."

"You should see all the skirts."

Benny waved to Rachael who was on the phone and left the Chief with a twinkle in his eye and a thought in his mind.

Vernon knocked on Big E's door and noticed sawdust and a small piece of trim, which had been swept off to the side. He remembered Benny saying he could tell there was some sort of struggle just inside the door. He also remembered Benny guaranteeing that Big E would have it repaired before anyone could question what happened.

Big E answered the door and his expression turned to fear when he recognized who was at the door.

"Good morning, Officer. I'm busy this morning, and I don't think my good friend Chief Neighbors would like it if he knew you were bothering me again."

"So be it."

"If that's the way it's going to be I will have to cut my donation to his re-election campaign with every question you ask that wastes my time."

"Good. Maybe I'll ask enough so you don't give him any money. I know somebody who might run against him next time who would be very happy if he didn't have his usual bankroll."

"And who would that be?"

Vernon put on the biggest and fakest smile he could muster. "What's with the sawdust on the ground here? Did you get some new door trim after somebody tried to force their way into your house?"

"No."

227

Vernon picked up the piece of discarded trim he'd seen on the ground and held it against the trim of the door. "Perfect match," he said.

"Is it illegal if someone breaks into your house?"

"No, but it's against the law and raises a lot of red flags when somebody doesn't report it and then lies about it."

"Fine. When my brother came back to town he tried to come inside, but I wouldn't let him. He tried to force his way in the house."

"Why wouldn't you let your own brother come inside? He's your family."

"He's bad news and all he ever wants from me is money."

"I thought he had a three million dollar trust fund."

"That's not true," Big E said, dropping his eyes. "I just said that to get you guys off my back."

"Would you like to tell me anything else you think I might need to know to find your brother's killer?"

"Not that I can think of."

"Why don't you tell me about the boat you were in the day I saw you at the Sleepy Cove Marina?"

"I was in that boat," he said, pointing toward the lake and a boat tied to the outdoor dock.

"No you weren't. You were in a smaller speed boat. I took a picture of the boat and its registration number. When I called the Georgia Department of Natural Resources, they were confused because the number doesn't even exist in their system. So, that boat either had a fake number on it or somebody knows somebody on the inside who wiped it from the system."

"Do you have a picture of me in *that* boat?"

Vernon just stared.

"Didn't think so," Big E said. "If you have any more questions for me, I would like to have my lawyer present so he can document your harassment."

Vernon continued to stare and simply nodded his head. Before he could finish turning around the door slammed.

Benny decided to swing by Red's to see how he and his houseguest were doing. As he approached the front door, hysterical laughter spilled out into the front yard accompanied with oohs and aahs. Red had told him on many different occasions he didn't need to knock, so Benny opened the door and stepped inside.

The guys were sitting at the kitchen table. They were looking at Ned's laptop and Benny could only see the back of the computer. They did not hear him enter the house as their eyes seemed to be glued to the screen.

"Have you ever seen anything so beautiful?" Ned asked.

"Red not having ever seen any so big. They is humongous."

"Look at this," Ned said clicking the mouse.

"My goodness! That the longest one Red ever see in he whole life."

"Well check out this juicy pair," Ned said.

"Oh my. Red mouth is water."

"What the hell are you guys doing?" Benny asked.

"You have to see the juicy ones, Bendy. Come look."

Benny hesitantly walked into the kitchen and to the other side of the computer screen. Two of the biggest, reddest tomatoes he had ever seen were on the screen.

"You guys are looking at pictures of vegetables?"

"Yep. Go to last picture," he told Ned.

A giant zucchini filled the screen.

"Nice," was all Benny could think to say.

"He showing Red giant watermeldons and squashes and all kind of giant vegables."

"A lot of crazy stuff on the Internet," Benny said. "How you feeling, Ned? Your face doesn't look as swollen."

"Oh, it feels much better. Red made a salve for me. It smelled awful, but after he smeared it all over my face and let it sit for thirty minutes the swelling all but disappeared."

"Red mama teach him."

"Do you feel safe here?" Benny asked.

"Yeah. When we go outside we're staying in the backyard so nobody sees me."

"You ready to tell me what this is all about?"

"No. I'd appreciate it if you'd let me handle it my way."

"Well, so far you've been doing a bang-up job of that," Benny joked. "Let me know when you're ready to talk about it."

"It's going to work itself out in the next day or two."

"That sounds a little cryptic."

"Thank you."

"Should I be worried?"

"No."

"OK. Let me change the subject. What do you know about Nina's ex?"

"He couldn't handle the pressure of the Oglethorpe name for one. I don't know if the drinking problem came first or the shame."

"Wasn't the plantation already in a pretty steady decline when he came around?"

"Yeah, but when each new generation was born they were expected to pull the family out of the tailspin and save the place. He didn't have the business sense to do it. Rumor has it that he married Nina for her brother."

"Wait. He married Nina for Uncle Karl?"

"Yep."

"Why?"

"Before Uncle Karl lost it, he was a pretty smart guy. Did he ever tell you about his ice cream invention?"

"No, but that explains the obsession with ice cream."

"He supposedly invented some kind of ice cream treat that was going to revolutionize ice cream and make millions upon millions of dollars. He worked on his idea for years and if you ask some of the old-timers around town they probably tried some of the test batches. Nina's ex, Phillip, crossed paths with Uncle Karl and saw the invention as his way to riches. He romanced his sister and got Nina to fall in love with him. He said he would finance the ice cream operation."

"Did he have money?"

"I don't think so."

"And it obviously didn't work out?"

"No, it didn't. Uncle Karl got obsessive. He claimed something in the recipe was off and he wouldn't show Phillip the recipe until it was perfect. In the meantime, Phillip and Nina had a baby. Uncle Karl worked on his art while he thought about his recipe, and he mentally slipped away."

"So, Phillip just got fed up and left?"

"Yep. He stole the recipe book and took off."

"Do you think he could be the one behind the murders?" Benny.

"I doubt it. He was awfully bitter, but it doesn't make sense killing strangers to get back at someone for not bailing you out of your hopeless life."

"No murder makes sense."

"Bendy." Red stood up. "Talk to that man."

"Red, he lives in Tennessee. It'll take me five hours to get to him. There and back is half a day wasted."

"It not wasted. Red get little bumps on he arms when he name is sayed. He know you answer."

"Red," Benny tried, "I know you've helped me solve my last two cases, but I don't have time to drive up there and back to question a man that hasn't been to this town for years."

"Red mama one time say to Red to listen to talking world for answer. Red mama say she can see answer since she not hearing them."

"I'm not really sure what you mean, buddy."

"Bendy not coming here today to hearing about Phillip, but he do. Bendy must not be going on and forget. Listen to talking world. Phillip bees important."

"Oh, Red. God I love you and you better be right."

"Go," Red said. "Go!"

Chapter 27

"Can you meet me at the boat for lunch?" Benny asked Vernon on the phone.

"Yeah, we really need to exchange notes."

"I'll meet you there in thirty. Do you mind if Rachael is there?"

"Of course not."

Benny picked Rachael up at the police station. On the way to the boat she tried to apologize again for leaving him for London. Benny told her he wouldn't hear it and told her once and for all to bury the topic. She nodded her head, hid a tear, and buried it.

On the boat, Benny took some chicken breasts out to the grill while Rachael tore up some lettuce and cut up some veggies for a salad.

"That smells good," she called to him. "What did you marinate those in?"

"Italian dressing," he called back. "Can you come out here a minute?"

Rachael put down the knife and walked to the outdoor deck.

Benny maneuvered the chicken breasts with a pair of tongs and placed them on the grill. The chicken sizzled.

"I'm headed to Tennessee after lunch to question somebody. I probably won't be back until two or three in the morning. I would love it if you could come along."

"Who are you questioning?"

"Phillip Preston. Red says I have to."

Rachael giggled. "Didn't he sort of provide the missing link for your last two cases?"

"Yes."

"You better listen to him then. I'll call Chief Neighbors and tell him I need to take the rest of the day off. The phone hasn't rung as much since we had the news conference."

"I didn't get to see it. How did Vernon do?"

"He's a natural. He must've had a good teacher." Rachael leaned in for a kiss.

"Please!" Vernon said, emerging on the outdoor deck. "If I'd known it was going to be this kind of lunch I would have gotten a Whopper or something."

"It's not going to be that kind of lunch," Rachael said. "I was just telling Benny how well you did on national television. It's not so scary, is it?"

"Not if you don't think about it. It's hard to get it off your mind at first. When I spoke my first sentence, I saw a million people watching their televisions. It was almost as if I was watching myself talk from somewhere outside my body."

"I've heard a lot of people say that," Rachael said, stepping away from the grill and a puff of smoke. "It usually goes away pretty quickly."

"It did," Vernon confirmed.

"I'm going to finish tossing the salad while you guys talk."

Vernon told Benny about his conversation with Big E and how he denied being in the speedboat with the mud on the front.

"But we both saw him in it," Benny said, sliding over one of the chicken breasts and repositioning it away from the flames.

"He said to prove it."

"I don't think it matters."

Benny told Vernon about the kid who drove the ice cream truck and the strange conversation he had with Big E about dirty boats.

"Did you say dirty boats?"

"Yeah, boats. As in more than one."

Benny told Vernon what little he knew about Ned's involvement.

"Ned wouldn't do anything like that," Vernon said.

"And I think that's exactly why his face is all busted up."

Over lunch Benny explained how he and Rachael were going to take a quick drive to Tennessee to check out Phillip Preston. Vernon agreed that it couldn't hurt, and promised to look in on Ned.

The drive to the small town in Tennessee took a little under five hours. The conversation for the most part was light. At one point, Rachael did ask Benny a serious question.

"Do you think you'll always live on your boat?"

"I haven't really put much thought into it."

"Did you see what just went on the market across the street from Red's house?"

"Yeah, the Thompson place."

Benny turned the radio to a different station.

"Birdsongs *would* be small for two people to live on day after day," he said.

Rachael nodded her head and turned up the volume on the radio.

Phillip Preston lived in a mobile home positioned in front of a large storage facility. A billboard above his home displayed a rocket heading toward earth and the words, "Inner Space—Your First Month is Free." A smaller sign in front of his trailer stated an attendant was on duty and guarding the premises around the clock. The sign had a picture of an astronaut waving.

As they got out of the Jeep, Phillip walked out the front door.

"First month's free if you sign today," he said, as if he was reading a script. "We have units for forty, seventy-five, and a hundred a month. You'll get a code to the gate behind me and rent's due by the fifth of every month." He hadn't looked at either of them once.

"We aren't interested in storage, Phillip," Benny said.

His eyes popped with Benny's usage of his name.

"Hey, I haven't missed any payments and was only three days late on the last one."

"We're from Tilley," Benny said.

"Oh. You two the law?"

"We're working the case in Tilley."

"Haven't heard about it."

"That's hard to believe," Rachael said. "Don't you have a TV in there?" She pointed at the mobile home.

"I have a TV, but I don't have the cable or satellite to go with it. This job doesn't pay for much more than the place to stay."

"If you really don't know what's going on in Tilley, why haven't you asked if your family is OK?" Benny asked.

"We're not real close. But I guess you already knew that if you came this far to find me. Is it against the law if I don't care how they are?"

"I guess not." Benny paused as the gate opened. It squeaked and made such a racket that Phillip wouldn't have been able to hear his voice. When the gate closed and the car passed, Benny continued, "They're all fine."

"I'm so relieved," Phillip said, deadpan. "Now, what do you want?"

"When's the last time you came to Tilley?" Benny asked.

"Probably been ten years at least."

"And you're sure you haven't been there at all this week?"

"I haven't left the property other than to go to the convenience store and maybe the grocery store once or twice."

Rachael's phone chirped and she walked away from the conversation to take the call.

Benny stepped closer to Phillip and continued.

"Do you feel as though you have any unfinished business in Tilley?"

"No."

"Let me get this straight. You married into a beautiful plantation house with lots of land. They have a well-respected family name. And you go from all that to living in a mobile home in front of a storage facility with little or nothing to your name. And you're not bitter? You don't feel cheated and want some sort of revenge on somebody?"

"No! First of all, that beautiful plantation house you were talking about has been falling apart for years. Last time I was there the paint was peeling off the walls. The air conditioner had been broken for so long and the humidity in the house was so high that the floorboards were warped. We had sold so much land that we basically were down to nothing. It was an embarrassment."

Benny nodded, hoping he would go on.

"I guarantee you I'm safer living in a mobile home than that place. And I don't have to live with the eyes of the town on me thinking that I'm such a failure. That well-respected family name you were talking about is the distant past. That family name now means loser, failure, incompetent, bunch of..."

"I get it," Benny said, stopping him from going on a rant. "Tell me about the ice cream recipe."

"Is that what this is all about? So I stole Karl's stupid recipe. Yes, I did that. It didn't do me any good because the stubborn bastard wouldn't finish it. I thought I could and I tried countless ingredients. I even tried to sell the unfinished idea to a few different companies. I had a few bites but nothing panned out. As you know, the people associated with that house of late aren't much in the way of business people."

"Do you mind me asking what the idea was?"

Phillip's eyes bubbled. "Ice cream cupcakes. Take a cupcake made with the most delicious yellow cake mix you can imagine. Inside of that is homemade chocolate ice cream and it's all topped off with a chocolate icing that is so good you would go weak in the knees. You know how you go to a birthday party and they always serve the cake with ice cream?"

"Yeah."

"Do you eat the ice cream and cake separately?"

"No, I like to get cake and ice cream together in the same bite."

"Exactly," Phillip said. "This was all that in one bite."

"It sounds like a pretty good idea."

Rachael ended her phone call. As she walked back she noticed a soft drink can on the ground. Remembering the game she played as a kid, kick-the-can, she gave it a good kick. A few bees had been sipping on the left over sugar and before she could jump out of their way, two yellow jackets stung her on the ankle.

"Ah, crap," she said stumbling over to Benny and slumping into him. "I got stung."

"Bring her in the house," Phillip said. "I've got some tobacco we can put on there."

Benny sat her at the kitchen table. Phillip pulled a cigarette out of a pack. He ripped off the paper and dumped the loose tobacco on the table.

He pinched some together, quickly ran it under the faucet, and handed it to Benny.

"Squeeze some of that juice and hold that on there. It sucks some of the toxins out."

"I always wondered if this really worked," he said.

Benny placed the wet tobacco on Rachael's ankle and within seconds the tension in her face and body eased.

"It does work," she said. "Thank you."

"You look familiar," Phillip said.

"I used to be on television," Rachael answered as Benny continued to focus on her ankle. Changing the subject she said, "That's a beautiful painting."

Benny's head jerked around as Phillip walked over to the canvas hanging on the wall.

"Yeah, she's certainly talented. She sent it to me about a year ago trying to reconcile or something. She's definitely the most talented artist in the bunch."

"Who?" Benny asked.

"My daughter, Angel."

Chapter 28

"Angel paints?" Benny asked as he tried to keep his voice calm.

"Like I said, she's the most talented one in the family."

"You said she tried to reconcile with you last year, why?"

"She's one of the reasons I left. She had been talking all kinds of crazy stuff like she was going to burn the house down and get it rebuilt with insurance money. One time, when she was having an unusually violent tantrum she told me she was going to kill me and collect what was rightfully hers. All that happened about the time Karl was getting weird with the recipe, so I took it and left town. I thought she might have felt bad about all the crazy things she said to me."

"You didn't write her back or call?"

"I did. You have to remember that was all about ten years ago and Angel was only twelve years old. First thing out of her mouth was a question about the recipe and if I had found a buyer. She didn't care about me. She cares about money and getting that house fixed. I was embarrassed by it, but she was mortified."

"Do you think she could be responsible for the things going on in Tilley?"

"You never told me what was going on."

"I figured you really knew and were lying."

"Turn on the TV, see for yourself. I don't watch it, don't read papers, and don't have many friends."

Benny gave him a quick version of the murders.

"Sounds like she's tired of waiting to get the house fixed. Show one of the paintings you found to her mother. She'll know if she painted it or not."

"I already did," Benny said.

"And?"

"She turned white and ran out of the room."

"I think you have the answer you came looking for," Phillip said, grabbing a cigarette.

"We have to get back to town," Benny said. "Do me a favor, don't call anybody or talk about this for a few days. Especially don't tell Angel. I don't want her to know that I know."

"I don't have a phone either."

"Perfect," Benny said, helping Rachael to her feet. "I'll be in touch."

"Don't trouble yourself," Phillip said, taking a bottle of booze out of the freezer. "Like I said before, I don't really care."

Speeding down I-75 south heading back to Tilley, Benny's phone rang. It was Vernon.

"I just checked on Ned and it seems like those two are having a blast."

"Were they still looking at vegetable porn?"

"No, Red was making grilled cheese and tomato sandwiches for dinner."

"It's ten o'clock at night."

"Don't shoot the messenger. And Ned was on his computer laughing hysterically about something. He made me promise if he went missing in the next day or two I would drag the lake looking for his body. I asked him if it had anything to do with Big E and he laughed harder."

"What do you think he's up to?"

"I don't know. Ned doesn't seem like the type to seek revenge, but he sure was beat up badly."

"He already acts like he has brain damage," Benny joked. "We'll be back in town a little after midnight. Probably close to one. I think I know who did this."

"Who?"

"Angel Oglethorpe."

"What?"

Benny explained to him what happened in Tennessee and the conversation he had with Phillip.

"You need to somehow make sure she's home and make sure she stays there."

"I drove by Rene's earlier and she was working. There was a pretty good crowd inside. I bet she's working until close. I'll find out and make sure she goes home from there and stays."

"Good. We'll put our heads together when I get back and maybe we can arrest her in the morning. I want to make sure it's a surprise and she doesn't have time to cover her tracks."

"Yeah, we certainly have to make sure the arrest sticks."

"I'll call you when we're about twenty minutes away. Looks like an all-nighter."

"I'll be ready."

Benny's phone rang at about the same time he smelled the smoke.

"The huge service bay at Big E's marina is on fire," Vernon said as Benny answered. Vernon was out of breath. "We just got a call requesting all the help our county could offer theirs."

"Must be a big fire. We're about five miles out and we can smell the smoke." Benny paused as Vernon yelled directions to one of the deputies. "We're starting to drive into smoke now. What have you heard?"

"Rumor has it Big E was servicing a lot of the boats he rents out and had them all docked at the indoor service bay. Somebody else claims they heard an explosion."

"What about Angel? Who's keeping up with her?"

"Nobody. We lost her. Somebody called Rene's about the fire and when word got out, people scattered. So did she."

"Dammit."

"I need you to drop Rachael at the station to help me with the phones. Then you can make an excuse to go over to the Oglethorpe's and lay eyes on Angel."

"It's nearly one in the morning."

"You'll think of something."

Benny dropped Rachael at the station. He racked his brain as he drove toward the Oglethorpe's trying to decide what to say as to why he was bothering them so late. As the house came into view he decided to lie and to say Rene was worried sick that Angel disappeared and she hadn't been able to get in touch with her. By the time Angel had time to validate the story it would be too late.

Benny rang the bell and knocked in case the bell didn't work. He waited and listened for footsteps. Not hearing any he decided to walk around the house to see if any lights were on. The lights in Nina's studio were blazing.

Sheers covered the windows, but Benny could tell someone was in the room. Benny rapped his knuckles lightly on the glass. The figure inside stopped for a moment before walking over to the window.

"Who is it?"

"It's Benny."

The window lock clicked and opened. The sheers separated and Angel appeared. She had yellow paint on her forehead.

"What are you doing?"

"Rene said things got crazy at the café and didn't know if you made it home safely or not. I promised I would check. She said with all the crazy stuff going on in town she wouldn't be able to sleep until she knew you were home and safe."

"Oh. That's nice of her. Tell her I'm here. I was just about to go to bed. I noticed mom left the lights on in here and was just shutting everything off for her."

"Glad you're safe. I'll see you tomorrow."

Angel shut the window. When she turned around she caught her reflection in a mirror and froze. The large yellow streak of paint across her forehead was impossible to miss. She gritted her teeth. Angel was certain Benny knew.

Chapter 29

Benny walked around the house just in time to see his Jeep speed down the long driveway. He regretted stopping to say hi to Clarice the ostrich. He dialed Vernon on his cell.

"I'm gonna need a ride back to town."

"Did you break down?"

"No, Angel stole my Jeep. She knows we know."

"Where do you think she's going?"

"Probably out of town. Come get me and we'll figure it out."

"Can't. You wouldn't believe how crazy it is up here. The smoke from the fire is blowing this way and people are scared. I'll let Ned have the keys to my car. He can come get you."

"Ned?"

"Yeah, he just came up here to make a confession. I told him I didn't have time right now. You can take his confession on the way back to the station."

Benny shook his head and slapped his free hand to his forehead.

"OK."

Benny heard the siren first. A minute later he saw the blue lights. Ned turned both off when he saw Benny's face.

"Do you really think that was necessary?" Benny scolded.

Red leaned over from the passenger side and said, "Yep, it be necessary. He the baddest driver I ever ride with."

"Get in the back," Benny said. "Let's get out of here before Nina and Uncle Karl come out."

On the way back to town, Ned confessed.

"The fire's my fault," he began. "Big E somehow knew I could hack websites and databases. He wanted me to change some numbers for him dealing with boats. He beat me up and said if I didn't do what he asked he would kill me. And I believe him. I almost changed the numbers for him, but Red changed my mind."

"Ned not a bad man. He a good man."

"And Red reminded me that I wouldn't be able to have a mushroom garden in prison."

"That would be a travesty," Benny said. " So, what'd you do?"

"This be the bestest part," Red offered.

"Oh, no. What did you do?"

"Since he tortured me in a way I thought I would give him a taste of karma and torture him back." Ned rubbed his hands together. "I composed an email that I addressed to the head of the United States Coast Guard, and the FBI, revealing all the numbers of the stolen boats and where to find them. I wrote a simple program on my computer that is counting down to zero, and when it gets there, it will automatically send the email."

"Like a bomb," Benny commented.

"Yes indeed," Ned said. "I sent Big E a video message earlier so he could see it."

"That's evil, Ned. I like it."

"Thanks. I figure he's trying to cover his tracks, and then he'll be coming for me."

"The night just got a little more interesting," Benny said.

The tiny Tilley Police station was a madhouse. Dark smoke drifted across the parking lot. Townspeople and media milled about clamoring for information. Both parties assumed the smoke had something to do with the murders and all wanted some clarity and comfort.

Benny asked Red to turn on the police car's blue lights as they entered the lot. The sea of people parted allowing them to enter and park. A throng of anticipating faces waited for them to get out of the car.

When Benny stepped out, the owner of the marina, Donny asked, "Now what in the blue blazes are you doing back here so fast?"

"What do you mean?"

"I just came from the marina and I saw your houseboat motoring away. I figured you were heading to check out the fire."

"I'll be damned," Benny said, realizing his boat had just been stolen by Angel.

Angel steered the boat away from the marina into the darkness. She watched the lights from shore as she tried to gauge how far she would be able to swim back. Angel killed the motor when she reached the point she decided was her limit.

Down below in the living quarters, Angel picked up a metal sculpture off Benny's coffee table and threw it into the sliding glass door. The first toss bounced off the glass leaving deep fractures that splintered like a spider web throughout the door. The second attempt sent the sculpture crashing through the glass to the other side. Glass rained down.

She yanked curtains and blinds violently from the windows slowly working herself into a rage. The screws holding the hardware for the window treatments came out as well, pulling chunks of the wall with them, which fell to the floor.

Angel dialed Benny's cell.

"Hello," he answered.

"You missing something, yet?"

"If you wanted me to take you for a ride you just had to ask."

Angel walked into the kitchen and opened the first cabinet she came to. Glasses filled the shelves along with a few expensive flutes. She picked one up and smashed it against the wall.

"I think you dropped something."

"Come on down to the marina, I have something I want you to see."

Benny motioned to Vernon and held his hand over the receiver.

"Angel's on the phone," he whispered. "Drive me to the marina." Taking his hand from the phone he said, "I'm on my way."

"I'm putting you on speaker," Angel said. She flung the rest of the cabinets open and started emptying the shelves. She swiped her arm across a line of coffee cups and pulled stacks of plates to the floor.

"Stop!" Benny yelled into the phone. A flash of rare anger hit him and he pounded his fist against the dashboard as Vernon drove.

"Do you remember when you told me that living on this boat was your slice of heaven?" Angel opened the fridge and tossed salad dressing bottles and other condiments onto the floor.

"I do remember saying that," Benny said squeezing his fist tight, trying to slow his breathing and calm down.

"Mine was going to be the Oglethorpe house rebuilt."

"Is that worth killing for?"

"Do you have any idea how humiliating it was to grow up in that house?"

"No, I don't, but I can imagine."

"No you can't," she said, throwing a potted plant onto the couch.

Across the lake, Big E paced in front of his office window. He knew burning the boats was a knee-jerk reaction, and in his panic he'd made a bad decision. He turned the television to an all-night news channel to see if the media was still covering the fire. They weren't covering the fire, but they were live, covering the frenzy at the Tilley police station. On the television screen he saw a lanky reporter bent over interviewing a frightened woman. Behind the reporter, in the background, he spotted Ned.

Without thinking what he would do when he reached him, Big E ran for his boat. He wanted his hands around Ned's neck. The quickest way to the

Tilley police station was to drive straight across the lake.

He pulled his cell phone out of his pocket and dialed Paul. He hoped Paul was at his girlfriend's house. She lived near the Sleepy Cove Marina.

"Hello," Paul answered.

"You asleep?"

"Yeah. You told me to act normal. I had a few drinks at my girl's house and fell asleep."

"Perfect. Pick me up at the Sleepy Cove Marina in five minutes. I found Ned."

"OK, boss."

Big E untied his fastest boat and cranked the engine. It purred with a deep power. Turned around and pointed in the correct direction Big E unleashed the power as he pushed the throttle forward as far as it would go. The bow of the boat sped forward, parting the glassy calm of the dark water.

"Are you at the marina yet?" Angel asked.

"Almost," Benny answered. "Will I be able to see you from there?"

"You better believe it," Angel said.

She began pouring liquid onto the floor and Benny could hear the splashing and gurgling of the container.

"What's that noise?" Benny asked.

"Oh, just five gallons of gasoline."

Benny didn't say anything. He didn't want to but accepted the fact that the houseboat he loved was a goner.

"I have three more of these containers. Lucky for me somebody had filled four of them and left them on the side of the office."

"You're going to kill yourself," Benny said. "I hope you didn't turn on the propane grill."

Angel spied the grill through the shattered glass door and quickly wheeled it into the boat. She pulled it into Benny's bedroom, turned on the gas, and shut the door. Back in the main room she emptied the remaining gas containers. She poured gas on the furniture, the tables, the crumpled pile of curtains, and anything else that crossed her path.

With a little less than half a container of gas remaining, she drew a trail to the outside deck. The plan was to light a cigarette, toss it onto the gas trail, and dive. Once in the water she planned to swim as deep and far away from the boat as she could with one breath.

"I'm here," Benny said into his phone. "I don't see you."

"Give it a minute. I just turned off all the lights. I'm hanging up now. Enjoy the show."

At the back of the boat, Angel put a cigarette in her mouth. She didn't smoke so the tobacco tasted foreign on her lips. She flicked the lighter, held it to the end of the cigarette and inhaled. The end of the cigarette lit up a fiery red. Angel blew the smoke out as her ears perked. She heard something.

Big E saw the lights of the Sleepy Cove Marina in the distance. The boat hummed at top speed and glided across the water almost as if it was flying. He put his hand on the throttle to slow down, but it was too late when he saw the strange cherry red light and the dark object in his way.

The speed boat collided with the center of the houseboat. The noise was deafening. The sight was spectacular. A scream of crumpled metal was followed instantly by a brilliant explosion of reds dancing with orange in a hellish twist that spun into the night sky. Fiery pieces shot across the water in every direction. Debris landed with the sound of waterfalls. Fire reflected off the waves made from the crash. The water shimmered and swayed. Almost as soon as it started the chaos was over. Slowly the sound died to nothing except the soothing roar of fire.

On the end of the dock, Benny and Vernon stood motionless watching it all. After a moment, Vernon looked at Benny who was biting his lip.

"You gonna to be OK?" Vernon asked.

Benny breathed out heavily. "Yeah." He put his hand on Vernon's shoulder. "My favorite ball cap was in there," he said.

"I'll get you a new one."

"Thanks."

Both men continued to stare out at the fire.

"Now what do you suppose just happened?" Vernon asked.

"I have a feeling we may have just wrapped up two cases without doing a thing."

Chapter 30

Two weeks later, bits and pieces of the bodies had been identified and the paperwork was almost complete. It hadn't taken long once the sun came up to figure out what had happened. The two funerals were over, and life in Tilley, Georgia returned to normal as the last of the national media vans drove out of town.

Benny and Rachael sat on the front porch of the house across the street from Red. The 'For Sale' sign in the yard now had a 'Sold' sticker across it.

Vernon arrived first for the housewarming party.

"I came straight from work," he said, handing Benny and Rachael a gift. "Connie and the kids will be along in a little while. Go ahead, open it," he said, pointing to the gift.

Rachael unwrapped the present and pulled out an Atlanta Falcon's ball cap.

"How did you know?" she teased. Rachael handed the hat to Benny who put it on his head.

"They say home is where you hang your hat and you didn't have one."

"It's perfect," Benny said. "Very thoughtful."

"Connie will probably bring something boring like a candle for you guys," Vernon said, winking at Rachael.

"Go on in and get a beer," Benny said. "Ned's already inside setting up a keg of his famous home brew. You won't hardly recognize him; his face isn't blue anymore."

Chief Neighbors arrived next with two dates.

"I couldn't decide who to bring so I asked them both," he said, laughing. He sent the girls inside to get him a drink. Whispering, although nobody was there to hear he said, "I told Vernon this morning that I'm not running for sheriff again and I gave him my blessing."

Rachael popped up out of her chair, wrapped her arms around him and gave him a huge kiss on the cheek.

"I would have done that years ago if I knew that's all it took to get a kiss from you." Chief Neighbors stumbled starry eyed into the house.

Uncle Karl showed up on a riding lawn mower.

"I brought you a present," he said, handing Benny a large black trash bag. "Open it."

Benny ripped the sides of the plastic bag open and pulled out the cowboy hat he had worn a couple times in Uncle Karl's studio.

"Oh, wow. I've gone from zero to two hats in five minutes."

"I know you love it—you almost didn't get it."

"I appreciate it, Uncle Karl. This really means a lot to me."

"Nina said to tell you she wouldn't be coming. She said she's going to be sad for a long time."

"Of course she is. I understand."

"She said to tell you thanks for the money."

Rachael looked at Benny. He shrugged his shoulders.

"The boat was insured. It was the least I could do."

As Uncle Karl disappeared inside, Red appeared.

"This is the bestest day of Red whole life, Bendy."

"It's a happy day."

"Red bring you some of he yummy tomato. You can go shopping in Red garden anytime you need."

"Thanks, buddy."

"Will you be Red neighbor forever?"

"I'm not going anywhere," Benny said, getting up and putting his arm around Red.

"Then Bendy and Red can stay here forever?"

"It sounds like a perfect plan to me. Let's stay right here forever."

Made in the USA
Lexington, KY
18 June 2013